Notable Places in Margaret Erskine's Journey

British or Indian Lands

Erie
Allegheny R.
Susquehannock
Juniata R.
Susquehanna R.
Fort Pitt
Philadelphia
PENNSYLVANIA
Monongahela R.
Potomac River
Baltimore
DELAWARE
Walnut Grove
Greenbrier Settlement
V I R G I N I A
Lewisburg
Union

N
W E
S

0   50   100
miles

TAKEN BY
the
SHAWNEE

Requests for permissions to make copies of
any part of the work should be sent to:
Turtle Point Press, 208 Java Street, Fifth Floor, Brooklyn, NY, 11222
info@turtlepointpress.com

Library of Congress Cataloguing-in-Publication Data
Names: Bingham, Sallie, author.
Title: Taken by the Shawnee / Sallie Bingham.
Identifiers: LCCN 2024002839 (print) | LCCN 2024002840 (ebook) | ISBN
9781885983367 (trade paperback) | ISBN 9781885983374 (epub)
Subjects: LCSH: Erskine, Margaret Handley Paulee, 1753-1842--Fiction. |
Erskine, Margaret Handley Paulee, 1753-1842--Captivity--Fiction. |
Indian captivities--Fiction. | Shawnee Indians--Fiction. | LCGFT:
Biographical fiction. | Historical fiction.
Classification: LCC PS3552.I5 T35 2024 (print) | LCC PS3552.I5 (ebook) |
DDC 813/.54--dc23/eng/20240223
LC record available at https://lccn.loc.gov/2024002839
LC ebook record available at https://lccn.loc.gov/2024002840

Print ISBN: 978-1-885983-36-7
eBook ISBN: 978-1-885983-37-4

Design by *the*BookDesigners
Map by Joe LeMonnier

First Edition
Printed in the United States of America

TAKEN BY
the
SHAWNEE

SALLIE BINGHAM

TURTLE POINT PRESS

Brooklyn, New York

TAKEN BY
the
SHAWNEE

AUTHOR'S NOTE

MY **FIRST CLUE** and inspiration for this book was a letter written in 1938 in Charleston, West Virginia, on the yellowing typewriter paper of the time. It is addressed in flowing script to "Master Worth Bingham" and "Master Barry Bingham"—my older brothers—from "Cousin Sally" who added, "I prefer the-just-Sally."

"I am sending you the story," Sally typed, "of your Great-Great-Great-Great Grandmother. Margaret Handley Paulee Erskine."

Sally added, "You must let your mother read it over to see if there is anything you should not read until you are bigger boys."

I was the youngest and a girl; Cousin Sally didn't consider me an appropriate recipient and yet I am the one who has read, studied, thought, and created, becoming part of the great modern movement of women taking charge of the writing of history.

These few yellowed pages contain Margaret Erskine's account of her taking by the Shawnee Indians in 1779, based on a brief narrative she dictated to her grandson Allen Caperton six decades after her capture in the wilderness on what was then the western frontier of Virginia.

By now, two hundred and forty-five years later, Margaret's story has passed through many hands and has been filtered through and colored by many points of view. Along the way, her voice has been lost. Her ignorance as a twenty-six-year-old white woman, her use of terms we no longer accept, her buried thoughts, her sighs, frowns, or sudden spurts of laughter were washed out, carrying away the intimacy of her experience.

Our expectations of that experience have changed as new light has been shed on what have been named "captivity narratives," nearly all by white women from different periods and different areas. Our expectations of these narratives reflect the agonizingly slow changing of our attitudes toward Native Americans. Now we know that many captives, especially the women, did not want to return to their earlier lives or their earlier families. Something in the tribal life they had experienced caused them to value it. Was it the friendships? The order? The shared work? The greater participation of women in the lives of the tribes?

Finally, a space has opened for my reconsidering and reimagining Margaret's life. I began this work as an ignorant white woman, a descendent of slave-owning colonists, just as Margaret began her story as an ignorant white woman imbued with the prejudices of her time and place. We have learned together, she as the actor in her story and I as the listening and learning author.

The story begins with Margaret's birth in Pennsylvania in 1753 and ends with her death in Virginia is 1842 at the ripe old age of eighty-nine.

Why should we care about Margaret's story? The courage and ingenuity she showed in surviving and adapting bear a similarity to the courage and ingenuity we all need as we face the relentless destruction of the natural world, a destruction prefigured by our destroying of native lands and traditions and peoples.

Courage, once it has taken root in a woman, endures, grows, and forms her future.

That courage shows in a portrait of Margaret painted when she was eighty-seven, two years before her death, by an unnamed itinerant artist. Wearing a decorous black bonnet, tied neatly under her chin, her small blue eyes gaze confidently. Her forehead is unlined and her commanding nose sits above a proudly pursed mouth that seems about to break into a knowing smile. A slice of silver hair shows beneath the edge of her bonnet and her organdy collar is decorated with trim over her white fichu. Although she was a small woman, her black-clothed body looks solid, a sturdy support for her remarkable face, all set in the nineteenth-century version of acclaim: a gold-leaf frame decorated with four clusters of embossed strawberries.

Margaret's gravestone, at the top of a hill in the Union, West Virginia, cemetery, looks out over the valley as though even in death she wanted a wider view.

This is the story of that wider view.

CHAPTER ONE

NEWS TRAVELS. Slowly. But it travels.

Scraps ride on canoes sliding down the Ohio, fly on the flèches of Shawnee arrows, burrow in packs strapped on horses carrying wanderers from Pennsylvania or the old coast colonies or heartland Virginia, where the land is worn out and crowded, or on hand-drawn maps in the pockets of farmers, woodsmen, ne'er-do-wells, craftsmen, apothecaries, disinherited sons, demobilized soldiers—and their wives and sisters and daughters—all gone West to see the lay of the land—the land of milk and honey: Kentucky—the promised land on the other side of the mountains, pierced by only one crossing, Cumberland Gap, where a wide buffalo-trampled trail—sometimes called the Warriors' Trace—leads at length and arduously to well-watered green prairies, land for the asking or just for the taking, according to the slowly traveling news.

By 1778 news had come to the little settlement of Greenbrier that Virginia's laws now allotted five hundred acres to each settler on the remote and dangerous frontier, with two hundred acres added for each slave brought west, up to a possible total of four thousand acres, all this to any white man who would journey over the mountains, plant a crop and put up a cabin and survey his boundary to establish his claim, and men who had served in the Indian wars could claim even more.

Margaret's husband, John Paulee, had fought White Bark and the Iroquois Confederacy in the Indian Wars in 1714. He had been awarded four hundred acres at Polly's Bend on the Kentucky River and began to nourish expectations. He knew he was owed more than the meager living he was scratching out on a small patch of nearly ruined land in the Greenbrier Settlement on the western edge of Virginia.

Early in the summer of 1779, John and Margaret had heard that D. Boone ("D. Boon," as he spelled it—it was said he killed a "bar" [bear] carved on a tree) had already explored the territory to the west and lived to tell the story of a land where every seed you put in the ground sprouted and grew. Boone had brought his family out to the fort at Harrodsburg and had survived captivity by the Shawnee. Now he was getting ready to depart on another expedition.

John knew neighbors who had already pulled up stakes and gone out with every relative and friend they could persuade, loading pack animals with household plunder, driving cattle and horses, whooping and waving as they left the Greenbrier Settlement—and all that summer wives and mothers, daughters, and sisters had listened to the stories, knowing their fate would soon be decided by husbands, brothers, or sons desiring more: more land, and better, more money from the sale of crops and hides, more risk—and that last was as potent an attraction as the first.

John had been complaining to Margaret that they were losing their chance for the betterment on which they had based their marriage three years earlier: not the hardscrabble life they had endured growing up in Virginia but the expansive hope and adventure of the West.

Now Margaret learned her fate: John said they were leaving on

September 23, 1779, a day after Boone and his party planned to go.

Margaret tried to draw him back. She never could be said to resist, but she reminded him that their first child, a daughter, so sickly she was not expected to live and so had not been named, was only a few months old and Margaret's milk failing. She reminded John of the horrors—bad news travels faster than good: it was only a year since Boone's son James had been captured by a Shawnee hunting party, tortured and tomahawked in the Powell Valley, his mutilated body left for his father to find and bury.

John told her that the time of such atrocities had passed. The war they now called Lord Dunmore's after the royal governor of Virginia, had been short and decisive for the tribes, with their defeat at Point Pleasant and the treaty of Fort Stanwix ceding their lands; the British, who had planned to seize those lands, were in retreat, and the French had also been driven off. Now, John told her, neighbors were pressing their claims to the good land on the other side of the mountains, and settled September weather would be perfect for their venture.

He had already cajoled his brother Alan and Alan's wife, Agatha, to come along. Two young men, Ben Goodall and Steven Shoemaker, not yet encumbered with family, had signed on as well. Safety lay in numbers, John told Margaret, who was still hesitating (he laid her unusual timidity down to her fear for her child), and with a party of six, four of them armed men, they would traverse the mountains in safety.

Margaret studied his face and knew she had no recourse but to accept. She'd seen him listening to the travelers' tales, not so much listening, Margaret thought—three years married but still notic-ing—as jumping at the news, grabbing it, strangling it like a baby bird—not that John would do such a thing, but he did have strong hands on the hoe and the pickax, although he was less certain on the flintlock, which he handled like a flower.

Later, much later, Margaret would think of that—the flintlock waving in John's hands like the too-long stem of a tulip.

From the day they met, she'd known John had the itching foot. He'd complained almost as soon as their cabin was raised of seeing smoke from neighbors, hearing the crack of axes splitting firewood, even smelling burnt corncob coffee every morning, acrid and strong.

This, Margaret disputed. She disputed very little else.

Now she began to prepare. Their old buffalo robes must be rolled up and secured with twine—she practiced on one, making sure to get it tight—their blankets bundled together, one feather bed mashed into a ball, tallow candles packed in saddlebags along with fire-flints, the griddle, the jerky from hams cured the previous fall brought in from the smokehouse, corn for the four cows and two horses hulled and packed in homespun bags she sewed herself, and with each task moving closer to September 23, she packed a prayer, a simple word or two: Lord, deliver.

Her husband, John, was not a Believer. Margaret knew he put his faith in the strength of his back, his swift running in moccasins, his weeklong hunts without sufficient food or water, the winter he was lost and kept himself alive in a hollow tree.

He'd begun in the evenings to fashion boots for Margaret, measuring each of her feet with his hand. The boots were soft deerskin, stitched carefully with a big needle and leather thong. John Paulee was good at such tasks.

Margaret also had her skills: a dab hand with a needle, all mending, sewing, and knitting easy and even a pleasure; tough slabs of venison soaked and simmered to perfection; her mother's knowledge of herbs and tinctures to heal every illness under the sun—but above all, and this she would not claim out loud—her smile, her laugh, the sunniness that shone every day as she sang at her work:

In Scotland town where I was born . . .
I gave my love a cherry without a stone . . .
There were three gypsies a-come to my door . . .

Equally precious although not equally prized by all were her book learning, her neat hand with a quill pen, the time she spent in the evening after chores reading a few pages of their two books, *The Pilgrim's Progress* and *Poor Richard's Almanack*. Her mother had seen to her children's schooling even in the wilderness, finding and paying a widow woman to put them through their sums and recite the lessons in their chapbooks.

Margaret had proved strong enough to endure her first labor and birth almost in silence, as she had promised herself. Nothing, she knew, would ever make her scream, not even, she believed, the agony of Boone's tortured son, begging the Shawnee to put him out of his misery.

But she knew for this journey she would need to be stronger still.

She began to haul pails of water from the town spring slung on a yoke across her shoulders, not only for her own family but for five or six neighbors. She labored to dig from the hard dirt of their garden patch the potatoes they would carry. She gathered all the blackberries she could find, dried them in batches on top of the wood stove, and mashed them with venison to make the hard pemmican they would soak in water to eat on the trail. Her arms and shoulders became stronger by riding every day, and she came to master her skittish bay mare, Jenny.

She liked to see herself at her tasks—it pleased her heart—her calico skirt flaring over her boots as she strode along, two pails swinging and dripping from her yoke. Her mother, Nancy, if she'd known, would have scolded her for vanity, but Margaret believed there were worse sins, although she could not have named them. Every night she washed her long arms and broad shoulders in a basin of water warmed at the fire, her skin pale and fine because protected from the sun, and when she had a moment, she brushed out her long light brown hair and admired her pointed face and blue eyes reflected in the pane of glass in the cabin window. John, catching her at it, smiled as though he knew that age and work would break her of all such displays, but Margaret was sure she would swing her skirts and brush out her hair even in the hard times they would encounter on the trail.

One evening as she rode through the home fields behind her cabin, memories of her father streamed back: how on their earlier allotment further south in Virginia he had offered her a crumb of the black ploughed earth on the tip of his finger, and she, a small girl trained to obey, had eaten it, not knowing what she was tasting for or why; and how, three years later, after they removed to the Greenbriar, he had offered her a crumb again and it had been gray and sandy-tasting. Seeing the face she made, he'd thrown his hoe on the ground—"Tobacco done ruint it!"—and never worked that field again. The tiny corn and squash seedlings he'd started wilted and died in the furrows during the hot summer. His death in a hunting accident had followed soon afterward.

Another evening she walked to Old Will's cabin, their nearest neighbor, to deliver his pail of water. She found the old man girdling a large sycamore at the edge of his home field. Dropping his ax when he saw her, Old Will complained, "Never come to this durned place to farm. Come 'cause gold was sprinkled on the surface of the ground, or so they claimed." He took her pail, emptied it into his trough, and thanked her curtly. "No more gold on this poor earth than back in Dorset, and now the durned tobacco took everything." Margaret passed on without replying.

Old Will's complaints were so familiar that no response seemed needed. She shifted her yoke to equalize her burden and turned on the footpath through the woods that led to the James Tyler cabin.

As she walked, she savored the new power in her shoulders, no longer galled as they had been at first by the weight of the rough wood yoke. Strengthened and enlivened by the prospect of change, she began to relish the oncoming adventure.

As she delivered her water to the Tyler cabin, she wondered if the day would come when this log cabin, hardly more than two sheds joined by an open dog trot, would be replaced by a brick house such as the ones she had seen on their trip up from lowland Virginia. Here the most substantial building she passed was Matthew's Trading Post, where she hailed a woman coming out with a bag of ground corn, delivered once a week from the grist mill across the valley. It was too early for the men to gather; later, after their work was done, a dozen or more would congregate to drink watered rum with sugar—bumbo, they called it—and play cards. It was a disorderly place and she was grateful that John seldom went there.

Next she passed the little fort, just a square of wooden fences with a watch tower at each corner. The previous fall they'd had to fly there after a scout came warning of an Indian attack: he'd seen a bunch of Shawnee coming up the Kanawha River, painted for war. The Greenbrier settlers had stayed in the fort overnight until it seemed the warring party had passed on down the river without stopping. That year had come to be called the Year of the Bloody Sevens because of the number of attacks, the Shawnee fighting back fiercely as they were pushed ever farther west.

Margaret had felt more than relief when they returned to their cabin. It was the first time she'd known she loved the place, small and poor as it was.

And now they were about to leave it without any hope of ever returning.

CHAPTER TWO

A S SHE FINISHED PACKING, Margaret whistled one of the old mountain tunes: *There were three ravens sat on a tree / Down a down, hey down, hey down / They were as black as black might be . . .*

Her mother hurried in, coming to help and supervise. She shrugged off her cloak and hung it on a peg with her bonnet. "A whistling woman and a crowing hen never come to any good end," she said, but Margaret knew it was more praise than censure.

Nancy watched Margaret packing her sewing supplies—scissors, thread, and needle—in the flame-stitch embroidered orange and brown housewife she had finished making the week before. "A stitch in time saves nine," Nancy noted approvingly. "John chose well when he chose you."

"Time will tell," Margaret said tartly. "This journey west will demand much."

"You always knew John Paulee had the itching foot," Nancy reproved. Her late husband had shared the same affliction. "Besides, in the end there's nothing here but work," she added, holding one of the big saddlebags open for her daughter to stuff in a blanket. Next went a quantity of clean rags for the baby, now sleeping in the cradle by the fire, as well as John's extra calico shirt and Margaret's linsey-woolsey gown and homespun apron.

"Even in the wild," she told her mother, "I mean to be as decent as possible."

"That choice will take you but a little ways," Nancy said, pulling the draw string on the saddlebag tight. "Work will take all your time and strength, nothing left for consideration of your appearance." But Nancy herself, Margaret thought, disproved the thought; even at hog slaughtering time, her gown was always spotless, her hair smoothly knotted up under her crisp bonnet. It was a pride in appearance they shared.

"But new stars in a new sky." From childhood Margaret had been a great sky watcher, even a counter of clouds.

"Remember what I told you, Daughter. Don't repine. Teach, Margaret, teach!" It was Nancy's daily refrain. Her daughter's book learning must not go to waste.

Nancy knew her book, raised by Pennsylvania Believers who wanted a Bible reader in the family. She'd told Margaret that her only hope of improvement lay in knowing how to write and do sums; otherwise, marriage at fourteen and as many as ten children. Book learning provided a girl's best chance of holding out for an older husband more likely to be able to provide. Margaret had proved her mother right. Marrying at twenty-four, she'd chosen John, who was solid and steady and wise in the ways of husbandry. She would never starve.

Nancy watched Margaret sliding the little almanack into the other saddlebag beside her sewing supplies and nodded approvingly. Regular reading of *Poor Richard's* sayings was a good and proper use of her education.

"I expect to see you put in your Bible," she said, knowing it was a vain hope. With no church of any kind near enough to attend, her children were growing up outside of the faith. Margaret did not need to answer.

The baby began to mew. Margaret snatched her up—her hunger was never timely—and sat down on the bench, opening the buttons of her shirtwaist, turning down her camisole, putting her left nipple between the baby's grasping lips.

But hardly grasping. She had to keep putting her back when she slid off. The baby weighed no more than a loaf of bread on her arm.

"Still sickly," her mother said. She'd lost her first two before their first birthdays.

"Cried all night." It was not a complaint, merely a statement of what all the women in the settlement knew. Margaret moved the baby to her right nipple, but the sucking was still feeble, her milk only a fitful stream, nearly as thin as water.

"Did you try my remedy?" Nancy asked.

Margaret recited the ingredients. "For costiveness: pignut, gentian, ginseng from John's big bag he plans to barter in Detroit, Indian turnip, the last of the tomatoes, boiled thick."

"But no wine?"

"We keep no wine here, Mother. You know how John disparages spirits."

Her mother pulled a small flask out of her placket. "Carry this with you in case of sickness." She handed the flask to Margaret.

Uncorking it, Margaret smelled the sweet, strong whiskey cure-all for woes of body and heart. She tasted it, made a face, and recorked it.

Her mother was grumbling, "No wine, no wonder my cure didn't work."

"She spit it up as soon as it went down." The baby was already asleep, a bubble of thin blue milk at the corner of her mouth. Buttoning up her shirtwaist, Margaret studied the baby's face, pale and round, a little moon with a speckle of rash across her nose.

Her mother bent to look. "The next one will be stronger."

"It may be, in a few years—"

"You know your duty, Daughter. We are sent to seed the wilderness. After you build your cabin across the mountains, be sure to fill it well."

Margaret said nothing. She knew her mother's opinion of a woman's duty. Married at fifteen, her mother was only twenty years older than her youngest daughter, and still in prime producing time. A widow with six children more than half grown, it was high time for her to marry again.

A knock on the puncheon door brought them both to their feet. Hazel Murphy, Tig's wife, stood on the doorstep, an infant in her arms, a child hanging on her skirt.

"You're back!" Nancy and Margaret were both staring. Hazel was scarecrow thin, her arms two sticks around her infant.

"God help us, let me sit a while." Nancy helped her onto the bench, Margaret ran for the kettle to make a cup of tea along with the last slice of gingerbread. Hazel slurped the tea and ate the gingerbread in two bites. "Those red devils!"

"They drove you out!" Nancy cried. Margaret knelt by Hazel, slid off her worn moccasins, and rubbed her blistered toes.

Hazel told them, "Eleven days they camped around the fort, firing their flaming arrows into our cabin roofs. Some caught on the shakes. I punched my share down from inside with a pole. But after ten days we had no water, no salt, a strip apiece of jerky. I told

Tig I'll not die here. It took some arguing. Nine days past, dark of the moon, we stole out of the fort, gathered the horses and the cows, took out over the mountains. Little Tig died of scrofula the third night, Tig dug a hole, buried him beside the trail with stones to keep off the wolves." She halted, rubbing her eyes with the back of her hand." We're back here now to stay." Her face, which had been rosy and plump, was withered down to a knob.

Margaret slid Hazel's feet back into her moccasins, asking, "The others— ?"

"Those fools stayed in the fort, even after Blackfish at the parlay spoke about a heavy dark cloud hanging over them."

Nancy helped Hazel to her feet. The child clung to her mother's skirt and the infant began to wail as they made their way to the door. Nancy opened it and the two women stood gossiping on the doorstep a while: who had been born, who died in the settlement in the seven months the Murphys had been gone.

Margaret began to gather what little was left for supper, their last meal in that place.

"Where will you sleep?" Nancy asked Hazel.

"Brother Wash till we get back to our own place—our cabin down by the creek, flooded I heard last April." Then Hazel and her children were gone.

"Never did have much sense," Nancy said. "Raising their cabin on the streambank, then lighting out from here in March before the last rains." She took down her cloak and hunched into it, tying on her bonnet with a snap of the strings and heading for the door. "I needs must be going, your brothers will be waiting for their grub."

"And Emily?" Margaret asked. She regretted that she had not left time to tell her sister goodbye.

"Oh, that girl, she'll be the death of me, off somewhere hunting acorns to feed her squirrels." Emily was the only occupant of the settlement who took pains to feed the wild creatures.

Nancy did not say goodbye. Farewells brought bad luck. She only laid a forefinger on her daughter's cheek. "Till morning."

At that, as though in answer, the fire began to smoke, filling the cabin with the smell of scorched pine sap. Margaret suspicioned the wood John had brought in was still green, cut in a hurry. She loved and resented her husband's hummingbird ways, how he picked and poked, jumping from one task to another before he'd completed the first, especially now in the haste of leaving.

"Leave the door ajar," she told her mother, waving out the smoke with her apron. Then she picked up the young rabbit John had shot that morning and skinned it, peeling back its hide. The raw pink called to mind her baby at birth. Scraping out the innards, she carried the offal to the door and slung it out for the dogs. Then she filled the big iron pot with water from her pail and swung it onto the hook over the fire. As the water heated, she began to chop carrots and turnips. The carrots called for another washing, dirt still hung in their beards, but she had no time to go again to the spring. No potatoes: John was saving all she'd dug for the journey, along with as many carrots and turnips as Margaret was willing to spare. She wanted their last meal to be plentiful, a blessing on their leaving, but there was hardly enough.

Last meal. Margaret didn't like the sound of it, remembering a lithograph a peddler had tried to sell her of the Savior eating his last supper with his Betrayer.

She threw a big pinch of salt into her pot and waited for it to simmer.

As soon as the water was popping, she picked up the raw rabbit by its hind legs and dropped it in, watching it flinch and curl as though it could feel the heat. She poked it down with her wooden spoon.

While the rabbit was boiling, she went back to filling the second saddlebag John had allotted her, in truth all her little mare, Jenny, could carry. The packhorses would carry four saddlebags, two on each side, with the heavier goods.

In went a big bar of her strong yellow soap. She'd made John promise they'd halt every noon by a stream or spring—the land they were going to cross was said to be well-watered—so she could wash out the baby's soiled rags and lay them to dry on a stone. If there was no time for that—John planned to keep up a steady pace—Margaret thought to spread the clean wet rags on Jenny's rump where they would dry as they rode. Sure to be patches of sun even in those dark woods.

In this second saddlebag she stored four loaves of salt-rising bread, wrapped in flannel, the carrots and turnips and a small bag of her remedies: yellow bark and alder bark and a handful of dried tansy, wrapped in a bit of cloth, to be boiled for fever or ague, a good spoonful every hour till the shakes came on. Shakes drove out the fever. She'd seen that cure work when her brother Samuel had been struck down in April—a wet, warm month, a fever month for sure—and shot up from his sick bed the third day after Nancy potioned him. Of course, Samuel was young and bull-strong. He'd petitioned John to go along on the trip West, but John had decreed that Samuel was needed at home to help his mother.

They might escape fevers, starting in September, a healthy month, dry and cool, before the late fall rains. Indian summer, they called it, because it was when the tribes went on the warpath. She'd tried to raise that with John, but he had hushed her, refusing to time their journey according to savage ways.

She went on packing her saddlebag. For aches and sprains, she shoved in a lump of bear grease in a paper quill, then a sack of meadow cabbage, lobelia and Indian hemp to boil up with honey, useful for all kinds of miseries. That reminded her to fetch her small crock of honey from the larder. Next she put in handfuls of blood root, garlic, and skunk cabbage, for croup. Her baby had nearly succumbed to a bout of croup a month earlier; Margaret had stayed up all night to dose her with this mixture. The baby, though feeble, had lived. Margaret planned to gather other herbs along the trail and dry them somehow. That was still to be imagined, then worked out.

For dinner, she threw the carrots and turnips into the boiling water with the rabbit. While she was stirring them down, Agatha Paulee, John's brother Alan's wife, came in, bringing an apron full of apples.

Margaret was very glad to see her. She had never called Agatha by that cold term, sister-in-law, loving her as a blood sister, as she was loved in return.

"Sit down with me, Sister," she said, "and we'll peel and core your apples, bake a Brown Betty if we can figure out how to carry it."

Agatha sat on the bench, took a knife out of her apron pocket, and began to peel an apple in a long spiral. "A basket in front of your saddle horn?"

"The baby goes there." Margaret sat beside her and began to peel another apple.

"I am grateful to the Lord I am not so encumbered," Agatha said.

Margaret said nothing. She would not repeat the gossip in the settlement that sooner or later Alan would put Agatha aside. A barren woman was not a wife, they said.

Agatha let her peel fall to the floor. "Remember when we were girls, we believed the apple peels would spell out our husbands' initials?"

"Foolishness," Margaret said, but then dropped her peel on the floor and studied it.

Agatha laughed. "That's no letter I've ever seen."

"I'll say it's a *J*," Margaret told her, although the peel looked more like a lounging snake with a curl in its tail. They worked in silence until half the apples were peeled. "You take these for your saddlebags and I'll load the rest unpeeled, they'll keep better," Margaret said.

Agatha pushed the unpeeled apples into the second saddlebag. She packed her apron pockets with the others. She glanced at Margaret. "Tell me truly, why are you setting out?"

"John wants it; he won't rest till we're on the trail, and I'll escape this cabin roof for a while, sleep on the dirt and maybe see the moon," Margaret said.

"Not much moon in those dark woods," Agatha said.

Margaret asked, "Why did you agree to go?"

Agatha shrugged. "The same," she said. "Alan will never rest till we get through the mountains."

The rabbit stew was boiling, filling the cabin with hot, sweet savor. Margaret skewered the rabbit out and began to sort the meat from the bones, nearly scalding her fingers. Then she threw the meat back in the pot and went to the door to toss the bones. "A benefit to the owls," she told Agatha. She didn't strew bones, usually. They were useful for making stock. But there was no time for stock-making now.

Agatha got up. "We start at dawn," she said, opening the cabin door. The men had set the hour of departure and there would be roaring if either of the women malingered.

Agatha gathered her things and departed. A minute later, John Paulee swung through the door, then paused, hanging by one hand from the lintel, his feet toeing the floor, a show of strength. He was wearing the leather hunting shirt Margaret had sewed and fringed for him. She looked at him, knowing he posed this way for her. Tall but narrow-bodied, which meant his extra breeches would not slide too far down Margaret's hips when she needed them for riding.

John hung a moment longer in the doorway, commanding her attention. "I saw a man clothed in rags, a book on his hand and a great burden on his back," he quoted in the voice of a backwoods preacher. "Where did you pack *The Pilgrim*?"

"Nowhere," Margaret said. "It's far too big to take along." She didn't mention the almanack, which was for her use only.

John sighed and sat at the table. Margaret spooned rabbit stew onto his plate and he began to eat. "Well, I did grant you governance over the packing."

"You know nearly every line of *The Pilgrim*," Margaret reminded him. "You can tell it to us in the evening by the fire. We will be needing some wisdom out there in the wilderness."

John reached across the table for her hand. "No repining, Wife. You know we must go."

Margaret took her hand back to spoon her stew. "I welcome the change," she said. It was nearly true.

Her sleep was broken that night when John flung his arm across her and cried out. After that she lay watching for the first pale light through the small windows.

As soon as it came, John jumped up, hoisted on his breeches, shuffled his arms into his hunting shirt, scuffed his feet into his moccasins, grabbled Margaret's two saddlebags, and lunged out the door. As soon as he was well away, Margaret took his second pair of breeches, which she'd hidden beneath the bed, and pulled them on. She planned to hike up her petticoat and gown once she'd clambered onto her little mare, then drape her skirts halfway down her legs, for decency. Taken up by their leaving, John might not make a commotion.

She lifted the sleeping baby and swaddled her, nestling her in the crook of her left arm.

Then she slung her housewife from her belt with the precious vial of pokeberry ink and the chicken feather quill. Her mother's small flask of whiskey she planned to tie to her saddle horn, knowing she would need to explain its usefulness in the case of illness. She would keep no secrets from John other than her almanack, her ink, and her pen.

Quickly, without a backward look, she stepped out and closed the door firmly behind her.

There was a cheering bustle in the clearing; three of the neighbors greeted her. Roused early, they were congregating to see the latest pilgrims on their way.

The men helped John and his brother Alan tie the cross sticks on the four pack horses, each set secured with breast straps. Then, two by two on either side of a horse, they heaved up the saddlebags and lashed them on. The horses shifted, adjusting to the weight.

Saddles went up next with mighty pulls on the girths—Margaret's mare flinched and kicked out till Margaret calmed her with a word. Last of all, the bridles. Margaret pushed the bit into Jenny's mouth to avoid the men's rough handling. Agatha's roan pony, Star, was saddled next. The two come-alongs, as Margaret tagged them, scruffy young men with no family in the settlement, waited, their packs on their backs.

Margaret and Agatha mounted, bundling up their skirts. Then John picked up his stick and shouldered his flintlock. Alan followed close behind him.

They were off, the horses stepping single file toward the start of the settlement trail that would lead them to its juncture with the Warriors' Trace.

Before they left the clearing, Mother Nancy came running after them, holding up a little bag. Margaret leaned down to take it and saw something strange on her mother's face. It was a tear.

"Godspeed," Nancy said, falling back.

Margaret opened the mouth of the little bag and smelled a mixture of her mother's special healing savories: a pinch of precious cinnamon, scarcely as much of cloves, a teaspoon of peppermint, all to be boiled up with honey and dosed for scrofula, cough, pneumonia, even consumption.

Nancy called after her daughter, "That is a good recipe. It seldom fails." Margaret tied the bag's string around her neck.

Then the little caravan disappeared into the trees.

CHAPTER THREE

I N A N H O U R, the sun came up clear and strong, melting the hoar frost as they rode toward the New River. They were following one of the settlement's dim trails that linked with the broad buffalo-trampled Warriors' Trace, leading to Cumberland Gap and the way over the mountains. Dark cedar and hemlock forest sealed the trail.

The horses plodded, saddles creaking, and Margaret regretted their slow going. The cows shuffled even more slowly. As the morning grew hot, sweat crawled down her back, and John's coarse britches chaffed her legs. "Might we proceed a little faster?" she called to John who was riding ahead.

He answered with a shake of his head. Margaret surmised that because the trail was thin and stony, the horses might stumble at a faster pace, even fall, heavily laden as they were. Behind them one of the come-alongs, walking, began to whistle "Coming Through the Rye" till Alan who was riding near him, told him to hush.

Soon the trail became so rough they were obliged to ride in the New River, shrunken by the past summer's heat; Jenny stumbled on an underwater boulder. On the bank behind them, the four cows bawled and refused to cross the water till a come-along struck them with his stick. Then they leapt in, wild-eyed, knocking against the horses. The splashing soaked Margaret's long skirt. The coolness was welcome but soon her skirt dried and stiffened and she longed to hike it up but feared that John would upbraid her. Later in the day when he might be distracted by other duties, she would give herself that freedom.

Out of the river, John set an even slower pace. Margaret's impatience was soothed by the salt smell of her mare's neck as the day, toward noon, grew unseasonably hot. Sweat stood in drops at the end of each of Jenny's dark hairs, then streaked and soaked in. Sweat crawled down Margaret's neck under her kerchief and she swiped at it and then at a marauding fly. Her hair, tightly knotted up, began to prickle, and she smelled herself, sour and strong. She was grateful that the baby in front of her on the saddle slept, rocked by the mare's motion.

Her saddle was ill-fitting, too high at the horn, and by midafternoon her thighs and woman place were raw. John glared when he rode back and saw she had trussed up her skirt to free her legs, visible now in his breeches.

"Cover yourself, woman," he told her, but she did not. Here in this tangle of trees and water she was freed of his command as she never was at her own fireside. He scowled and rode on.

She began to sing. "In Scotland town where I was born, there was a fair maid dwelling, made many a man cry lackaday, and her name was Barbara Allen." Riding near her, Alan, out of some vague sense of respect, did not hush her.

Now they were riding through a forest deeper and darker than any Margaret had seen. Many trees had been cut down for the Greenbrier Settlement and its adjoining fields, and she had never seen trunks as large as these; it would take four people, arms outstretched, to girdle them. She recognized black walnut, hickory nut, and chestnut, rare in the settlement, and remembered hearing that these trees had been planted years ago by the savages. From time to time, they had burned the saplings and the weeds springing up under the tall trees, and the soil under the horses' hooves was dark with ash.

The baby grew costive in the afternoon, tuned up, then screamed full blast till Margaret snatched her up and laid her to her breast. Not enough milk to fill her and she began to fidget and cry again.

"Keep her quiet," John ordered. "I have a thought we are followed."

After that the thickets bloomed with eyes. Margaret had seen the vagrant Shawnee when they passed through the Greenbrier Settlement, stopping at a cabin door and standing there until a piece of corn pone or a chicken wing was laid in their hands, then passing on, each foot planted in front of the other. Once when they had stopped at her mother's cabin, Margaret had stood close enough to smell them, smoky but milder than John's bear grease and dried sweat reek.

The baby fussed a little while longer, then fell into a fretful sleep.

Coolness came as they passed under the shadow of a great limestone cliff. Boulders laying beside the trail were coated with bright green moss. As they passed out of the cliff's shadow, they crossed an open space where enormous chestnuts stood guard, their exposed roots as thick as an elephant's foot. Margaret had never seen an elephant, but there had been an engraving on the wall of her school room.

Now the trail climbed up a hillside. In the valley below, Margaret saw a throng of sycamores stretching their limbs to the sky. The sight chilled her; the bare white limbs looked like scoured bones.

Jenny shuffled through a thick overlay of last fall's leaves and their pungent smell filled Margaret's nose and throat. She unleashed her canteen from the saddle and downed a drought. The water was warm and tasted of the canteen's tin.

In the afternoon Alan split off to hunt.

Evening came with a lessening of the heat as the sun lowered slowly behind a dark bank of trees. Soaking wet, the baby began to fret again. In spite of his promise, John had allowed no stopping to eat or care for the baby at noon, and when his brother Alan had frowned and muttered at the relentless pace, Margaret had remembered the long-simmering ill feeling between the brothers. She'd never asked to understand it, thinking it was something in the Paulee blood.

She loosened the soaked swaddling bands to give the baby some relief.

Agatha rode up beside her, hissing to calm the fretting. Margaret glanced at her sister, taking some comfort from her fair, round face, half hidden under her bonnet, and the hot glance of her small blue eyes.

"The first of our difficulties," Margaret said, rocking the baby with one arm.

But Agatha offered no sympathy. "We are pilgrims, starting out," she said, calling to Margaret's mind the evenings during the winter past when, after the chores were done, they'd sat close to the fire, reading from *The Pilgrim's Progress*.

Margaret fell into line. "From this world to that which is to come," she quoted; she had memorized whole blocks, finding comfort although she was scarcely a Believer. The memorized sections were good to repeat to herself when she was milking their lean and fractious cow. That animal and the three others, now far behind them, were crashing through trees along the trail, prodded, Margaret expected, by the come-alongs.

Agatha took up the text. "As I walked through the wilderness of this world, I lighted on a certain place where there was a den and laid me down to sleep."

Soothed by Agatha's voice, the baby found her thumb and slept at last.

"Please God we'll find a den to crawl into before dark," Margaret said.

"But you don't believe in Him."

"Necesse est," Margaret said, the only scrap of Latin she remembered.

Agatha sighed. "I'll settle for a fire and our buffalo robes spread close to it."

"I shook and beat and aired the skins before we left, but it did no good. They will make good bedding except for the nits."

"They'll bite like all the sins," Agatha said with a small laugh.

As darkness began to shroud the trail, John called a halt. Alan came back from the woods, empty-handed; they were still too close to the settlement, the woods had been picked bare. The two women dismounted and hobbled their horses. The come-alongs gathered the cows. They ladled out a few handfuls of cracked corn from one of the sacks, then fell to work assembling a sort of corral from fallen timber, herded the cows in and fed them. Watching, John nodded, satisfied.

Having decided to take the milking by turns, Agatha began, and soon had a brimming pouch of milk, more than they could use that night or carry, but essential to ease the cows and stop their bawling. The travelers took turns scooping milk from the leather pouch.

In the middle of the bare place John had chosen for their camp, Alan made a big fire with branches, twigs, and fallen leaves. John grumbled when he saw that in the windless air, the smoke was rising straight up, a sure sign of their presence.

The two women threaded bits of flesh from the fat plucked hen Alan had brought, roasting the meat on hickory sticks held close to the flames. The meat sputtered as it cooked, slinging sizzling drops into the fire. Margaret sniffed up the smell with pleasure.

Agatha took six biscuits out of her saddlebag, and Margaret dressed them with drips from her pot of precious honey. It was a feast, she declared to herself, seeing the long limbs of the men as they ate, stretched to the warmth of the fire, their leather boots beginning to heat and stink. She liked knowing that she and Agatha were surrounded by four good men, although she hardly knew the two come-alongs. But they looked hardy, backwoods boys who had long since learned to build fires, dress a horse's galls, stuff saddlebags, herd cattle, hunt, kill, and skin—and probably a good deal more. Perhaps even how to use their flintlocks in an attack, although Margaret noticed they had left their guns in a disorderly pile at some distance, along with their bags of black powder and bullets. She calculated how long it would take to reach a gun, load it, aim, and fire—too long to be of much immediate use, she thought.

John's and Alan's guns were scrambled with the rest. She remembered that John had said the treaty—she'd forgotten the name—had ended the long years of trouble with the Shawnee. Still, she murmured to Agatha, "They've left their weapons at a distance . . ."

Agatha shrugged, but John, overhearing, ordered the youngest of the come-alongs, a fair-haired boy named Daniel, to fetch his flintlock, powder, and bullets and lay them close by. Margaret wondered why John had chosen the youngest who, unskilled, might take a while to load his gun.

Noticing that she was looking askance at his choice, John explained, "I'll learn him."

Margaret said nothing.

Agatha gathered up the remnants of the meal while Margaret stripped and changed the baby, who for once lay quietly, looking up at her with pale eyes that would darken to gentian blue with time, if she lived. Margaret dried her with a rag before tying her up in fresh cloths and swaddling her. Before the fire was out, she had spread her buffalo robe, nestling the baby in a fold, then placing her saddle at the head. Jenny whickered, almost near enough to reach for a nuzzle. Her saddle's crupper was too high to use as a pillow, but the curve of it gave Margaret shelter as she said her prayers:

Now I lay me down to sleep.
I pray the Lord my soul to keep.
If I should die before I wake,
I pray the Lord my soul to take.

The words, learned when she was a tiny child, were comforting, even though she didn't know and couldn't imagine who this Lord might be.

John, stretched nearby, reached out to touch her foot with his by way of goodnight.

He was soon snoring, but Margaret, still awake, stared into the dark trees. The fire was shedding a little light from its last embers, and the shadows of the tree seemed to be marching, single file, toward the huddled sleepers. Margaret reached for her housewife and took out the almanack, her vial of pokeberry ink, and her quill pen.

Leaning on her elbow and slanting the almanack toward the firelight, she opened it to the first page.

She read, "A child thinks 20 shillings and 20 years are scarce ever to be spent," printed under the portrait of Mr. Franklin with the crease atop his nose.

Margaret had never seen twenty shillings all together in one place, and as to twenty years, her first twenty-seven had been spent at full speed.

She wrote in the small blank space under Mr. Franklin's words, "Started out, rode all day, raw and chafed, baby restless."

She turned back to the bare front page, just inside the cover, where she had written dates and lines.

JULY 3, 1779

My babe born four a.m. with Mother serving to help me. Midwife Susan Brown came in, her herbs did little. Sore nipples, little milk, rubbed with strong sassafras tea, some relief.

JULY 21

Baby poorly, croup nearly took her, Mother's potions pulled her through. John came in with big deer. Full moon.

AUGUST 8

Husband asked if I am prepared to travel. Baby cured of thrush. D. Boone passed by, taken by Shawnee two months previous in the Ohio Country, carried to their town on the Scioto River, received good treatment, adopted into the tribe, named Big Turtle. Speaks well of the Shawnee, talks of starting West again in September.

AUGUST 15

Still terrible dry. Corn crop burned up in the field. Neighbor James McKinley shot a buffalo, first one seen in many months. John says they are gone here, we will find them when we journey West.

SEPTEMBER 5, 1779

D. Boone stopped by again, calling for a group to leave for Cumberland Gap. Annie and Foster Williams gave their assent, then Babs Tucker the widow woman and Mark Thompson. Baby feverish but recovering. John told me we are to leave September 23, the day after Boone's departure. I wondered at our not going with his group. Husband said he preferred his own party.

It was enough. She closed the little book and returned it to her housewife with her ink and pen.

John was snoring louder. At last, she fell asleep to the drone.

CHAPTER FOUR

A T DAWN, when the clearing was still swamped in darkness, Margaret was wakened by the baby's wail and saw a single star to the east—Venus, she believed. As daylight slowly leaked into the clearing, the star winked out. She drew the baby to her and began to feed it.

Before she was done, Agatha was climbing out of her bedroll and shaking out her skirt. She searched the saddlebags for corn-meal, ground a few days earlier, to make the breakfast pone.

As Margaret fed the baby, she watched her sister's quick move-ments with appreciation. Already, Agatha was taking to life on the trail. She had always been hardy, even as a very young girl, a dar-ing tree-climber and loud singer; Alan's courting had not seemed to settle her. Margaret remembered how Agatha had laughed at his trials of tenderness—a pat on her shoulder, an arm, cautiously, around her waist—when other girls would have blushed with plea-sure, bowing their heads. Alan—bless his heart—had looked puz-zled, then he had smiled and drawn his hand away.

After that, the wedding had proceeded posthaste, as though his appetite was whetted. Lacking a church or a preacher, they had gathered one evening around a fire, drinking, singing, and even, she remembered, reciting some sort of prayer. And then the couple had marched off quickly to bed in somebody's loft.

But no baby had come out of that. It seemed a strangeness.

In her palm, Agatha was mixing the cornmeal with water doled out drop by drop from her canteen. She shaped the wet cornmeal into biscuits and laid them on the griddle over the fire's hot coals. Then she licked her fingers clean. Seeing Margaret watching, Agatha gave her a quick bright look. "Your task tomorrow."

"As we agreed." Margaret smiled with the pleasure of their association. Her four younger sisters at the Greenbrier had shirked most chances to work together. In their big family the youngest children learned early to disappear at chore time. Nobody had time or energy to round them up. The older children did what had to be done, Margaret shouldering most of the load, her duty, she knew, as eldest daughter.

Now the men were stirring, yawning, and stretching, waking to the smell of hot biscuits. John and Alan took two, Daniel and Tom, the come-alongs, seized one each, and the one biscuit remaining Margaret and Agatha split. A drop of honey from Margaret's hoarded flask gave only a little flavor, but the biscuits were filling. Then Daniel and Tom went to round up the cows and horses.

After visiting the thicket for necessities, the men began to load and saddle as Margaret and Agatha hurried to the thicket. Agatha grinned, seeing Margaret's breeches when she lifted her skirt. Returning, Margaret freed Jenny from her hobble, fed her a palmful of grain—the mare would drink at the next stream, where they could all refill their canteens—then heaved up her saddle. She tightened the girth till the mare turned her head to stare.

John came with two saddlebags and they lashed one to each side of Jenny's saddle. The baby went next, secured to the saddle horn. Sleeping, she did not seem to notice. Then John hoisted Margaret up, planting a small kiss on her cheek.

For that kiss, Margaret thought, she would pardon him anything, at least for the day.

Sunlight pierced the trees as they rode out of the clearing single-file; the cool morning air quickly warmed, and Margaret smelled the dryness of the leaves the horses were trampling. Now and then a lower branch swiped her face. The baby was quiet, clean, and dry, rocked by the mare's rolling gait.

She rode to the head of the company, relishing the silence filling in around Jenny's hoof clops. Then she reined in, hearing Agatha's call.

"How many days till we reach the gap?

"Alan thought fourteen or fifteen if we press on," Margaret said. "Today we'll stop at noon to eat. I told John it was necessary."

Agatha laughed. "And he agreed?"

"Said nothing but did not deny it.

Margaret was already thinking of the jerky in her saddlebags. Feeding the baby meant she was always hungry. "I could chew rawhide," she told Agatha.

"Half a biscuit's hardly enough. There'll be even less later on."

They knew what they were facing. Travelers' tales had streamed back through the Greenbrier for years, how one party had to kill and eat a horse or starve, another went to eating varmints. Some scandalous whisperers even said a sick baby had been killed, roasted, and eaten after three weeks on the trail and no luck hunting. So many people had passed through going to Cumberland Gap that the woods were picked clean of game. That, it seemed, *no one* starting out had expected.

"We'll tighten our belts," Margaret said, half believing it.

That started Agatha off; she was always a tease. "A nice fat wild turkey, roasted till the skin crisps."

"Don't!" Margaret's mouth was watering.

"Or a pair of catfish fried in a pan of grease."

Margaret swiped her mouth with the back of her hand. "You'll martyr me!"

Relenting, Agatha said, "Remember what Evangelist said to the man in despair?"

"Say it, Sister!"

"He said, 'Do you see yonder wicker gate?'"

Margaret searched the wall of trees on either side of the trail. "No."

"Do you see yonder shining light?"

Margaret craned her head to see a patch of sunlight on the trail ahead. "I do."

"'Keep that light in your eyes and go directly there to.'"

"What light, other than a patch of sun, are we aiming to reach?"

"The light that leads to the Promised Land, Kentucky, the paradise allotted us for our striving. the Land of Milk and Honey."

"The Shawnee don't call it that," Margaret reminded her. "They call it the Dark and Bloody Hunting Ground. Daniel Boone told us that when he was passing through."

"Savages," Agatha said.

At that word the two women fell silent, listening to the creak of their saddles and the clip of the horses' hooves as they passed over a stony patch. Now out of John's eye range, Margaret hiked her skirts up to her knees and pressed Jenny into a trot.

Behind her, she heard Alan begin to practice his owl hoots. All the boys in the Greenbrier Settlement learned owl cries to convey their whereabouts when they were hunting.

John shouted at his brother, but Alan went on hooting, then tried his wolf howls, real enough to make the hairs rise on the back of Margaret's neck—that dreadful lonesome wail. She pulled Jenny up and turned to look back. She saw John riding his brother down, grabbing his shoulder, clapping a hand over his mouth.

Then the two men tumbled off their horses, which took fright and lumbered off. John pinned his brother down and pummeled him. One of the come-alongs caught the reins of the frightened horses.

"Be silent, you fool," John gasped, holding his brother down.

"Hoot," Alan began, half choked. John pulled his ears.

"Hoot." It was fainter now. And then the beginning of that terrible howl.

John choked his brother till Daniel tore them apart.

At that moment, a shot rattled the branches by Margaret's head.

"Turn back, women!" John shouted.

Agatha turned her horse, but Margaret, her blood up—was it that heathenish howl?—dug her heels into Jenny and rode on ahead.

A hand snatched her right rein. She tried to free it. The hand jerked Jenny to a halt and then a pair of hands dragged her from her saddle. She snatched the baby up as she fell, protecting her with her arms.

And then she was on her back. The baby, awakened suddenly, began to wail, then tuned up to scream. She clutched the baby with all her strength, but another pair of hands pried her from her arms. She scrambled up and saw John and the other three men striking at five Indians, closing, falling on the trail behind her. No one had had time to load and fire. Agatha was fast to a tree, tied with a rope. She was screaming.

As John grappled with a warrior, Margaret saw a tomahawk raised over his head. John used the butt of his flintlock as a club, striking, and the savage reeled back then straightened, aimed, and fired. Clutching his side, John dropped his gun and Margaret screamed. She could see blood streaming from his side.

And then that smoky smell.

Now a face loomed above her, long ear lobes with an ornament, a feather topknot. The face had no expression she could decipher. He was holding the baby.

"Give her to me!" Margaret screamed. She felt herself grabbed from behind, her arms pinioned.

The savage flipped the baby, holding her by the heels and dashed her head against a tree. The sound was like a gourd struck with the heft of an ax.

Then he slung the body to the ground.

Margaret saw it crumple. She crawled toward it. Hands seized her, dragged her back.

The topknot Indian pulled her up and pushed her into her saddle. She saw Agatha untied and heaved onto her horse. Behind them, John was staggering away, then running, bent over, his arm tight to his bleeding side. Alan was on the ground, motionless, an Indian on top of him with a scalping knife. The two come-alongs had fled, leaving the horses and cattle.

The cows were bawling with hunger. One of the Indians took out his flintlock and shot each cow through the skull, smoothly and quickly. They crashed to the ground as Agatha, sobbing, protested, "Not poor Bessie!"

Margaret hushed her.

The Indians stared after John, who was still running crookedly. The one with the topknot who had killed the baby asked Margaret, "Captain?" She shook her head. Numb, almost paralyzed, she sat vacantly in her saddle. On her horse, Agatha was sobbing.

Their horses' reins were gripped by two of the Indians while the others snatched up their buffalo robes and guns, their pots and pans. One split the balled-up feather bed, scattering a storm of feathers. Margaret felt for her housewife and canteen, still lashed to her belt. She drew her cloak over them.

The Indians jumped on their horses. Topknot led the way, and the Indian behind Margaret prodded Jenny forward with his stick. She turned her head. The small patch of white under the tree—would the wolves find it that night?

She made herself stare at the brown back of the Indian in front of her. Her only hope lay in seeing clearly. A broad, muscled back, but there were folds of flesh drooping below the shoulders—an older man than Topknot, maybe his uncle, she surmised. Deep, crusted-over scars ran along his spine. His head was not shaved as Topknot's was. His hair was tied up tightly under a sort of bandana. Big hoops of wire dangled from his long earlobes past his shoulders, swaying as he rode.

She had seen those hoops before. Shawnee. The name that was whispered in the Greenbrier Settlement as though it was a curse, some even crossing themselves when they said it.

The Shawnee's horse, a black, white-splashed gelding, minced and balked at the shadows moving across the trail, but Uncle (as she decided to call him) rode with loose reins, easy in the saddle.

So, Uncle. She knew she needed to name each one of the war

party. She knew beyond reasoning that her survival depended on it.

She looked back, but she could no longer see her husband stumbling away down the trail. He'd seen her on the ground, the baby too, and must be thinking they were both dead. She knew there was nothing he could do for her now.

The come-alongs, she figured, could not have been expected to stay and fight. They would make it back to the fort with news of the attack, even if John fell along the way and a band of pursuers would begin to form. But Margaret had noticed that it often took several days for six or seven men to be provisioned, armed, and mounted. Meantime, she had only herself.

Riding behind her, Agatha was sobbing. No help there, Margaret thought with a flash of rage. And yet Agatha had seemed such a sturdy girl before she saw her husband lying on the trail, his scalp knifed off.

Suddenly Margaret remembered her flask of whiskey, still lashed to her saddle horn. By some miracle, the savages hadn't seen it. She knew from the tales of settlers fleeing back from the West that the Indians became even more violent after drinking liquor. Surreptitiously, she loosed the flask and dropped it onto the ground

Then she thought, *Well, there's the last of it, the last link*—then remembered her mother's little pouch of dried herbs, still hanging from the string around her neck. She touched it with her forefinger, feeling the rush of tears in back of her eyes.

For distraction, she made herself begin again to study the Shawnee warriors riding in front of her, skipping over Uncle. Ahead of him, two younger men, brothers, she decided, kneed their ponies into a trot. As they rode ahead, Margaret saw that one wore a sort of cap with a tall white feather sticking up and a leather coat such as men wore around the settlement. Booty, perhaps. His flintlock lay in front of him on the saddle. If he was the one who shot John, the flintlock would be hot against his thighs.

The other younger man, Brother Two, she dubbed him, glanced back, and she saw that he wore a small white ring threaded through his nostrils and two long strings with round pendants swinging from his ears. His black hair fell to his shoulders, fastened by a raven's wing ornament that reached from his crown to his nape. Raven Wing, she decided.

She heard Agatha yelp behind her and turned to see that a white man she'd not noticed had ridden up beside her sister and was prodding her mare with a stick. He wore a bunch of owl feathers on his shaved head, but she knew from his skin and features he was no Indian. He prodded Agatha's mare again in the belly and she flinched so sharply that Agatha lost her seat and fell. On her back on the ground, she pulled her skirt down over her knees.

In front, Topknot called a halt. No one looked back at Agatha. The white man, grinning, kneed his horse and rode off. Agatha's mare stood trembling by the trail.

"Get up!" Margaret shouted at her sister. She knew what would happen if Agatha failed to mount.

Sobbing, Agatha managed to catch her mare's reins and drag herself up into the saddle. Her bonnet had come off and dangled down her back by its strings, her fair hair, loosened, streamed, and her face was streaked with mud and tears.

"Ride beside me," Margaret told her. The trail was barely wide enough for two, but Agatha managed to come alongside.

"Stop crying," Margaret said. "They'll be more likely to leave you alone." She hadn't grown up with older brothers for nothing.

Agatha's left elbow was bleeding through her sleeve. Margaret tore a strip off her petticoat, and her sister managed with one hand to bind up the wound.

The party moved off. Margaret did not believe Topknot had called a halt because of Agatha. He was twisting his head, listening for something behind them.

Ahead of them, the white man reined in his horse and waited for the others to pass. As Margaret rode by, he looked at her and flicked his lips with the tip of his tongue. It was as dark as a leach.

Ignoring him, Margaret set herself to study their course. From the angle of the sun, she guessed it was not yet noon. A way's back, they had left the New River behind at its confluence with a larger stream that they were now following. Margaret calculated they were heading in a northwesterly direction. They were not traveling to Kentucky.

Then where? Fear came back to her, a renewed assault. The trackless wilderness. The back of beyond. The land of no return. She stared at Topknot's broad back at the head of the line. Their leader. She would learn to place a fragment of trust in that.

As though hearing her thought, Topknot spoke a word and the company broke into a trot. For a moment Margaret thought he might have detected pursuers, then she reminded herself that it was far too soon. They jolted along over rocks and fallen branches. Jenny jumped over nimbly, but Agatha guided her mare around, causing her to fall behind. Margaret motioned to her to ride up quickly. Now the white man was behind them.

They rode all day without stopping, till darkness blotted out the trail. Then Topknot, with a shout, called a halt. Margaret heard a stream running nearby and hoped for water. Hunger had left her, but she was parched. The men were jumping off their horses. Margaret slid down, then she helped Agatha off. Her sister was limp as a sack in her arms.

Margaret longed for a fire, but none was made. Brother One, as she had decided to call him, passed strips of jerky from her own saddlebag. He had thrust her leg aside roughly to lift the flap. Then the men stood around and ate quickly. Brother One shoved a strip at Margaret, but she pushed it away. Agatha reached for the jerky, tried a smile, and ate it hastily.

Topknot called to the white man. "Simon Girty. Water." Girty took their canteens down to the creek and filled them. Margaret sopped her dry mouth with the smooth, cold water. It tasted of mud and rocks.

When they had eaten and drunk, the men prepared for the night. Margaret noticed that they always made much of their modesty, retreating far into the woods for their necessities, leaving Girty as guard. He grinned at Margaret and made a sign with his fingers she could not fail to understand. She turned her back, gritting her teeth and clenching her fists. She would not make it easy.

Topknot dispatched the two brothers into the woods to hunt. Then he gave an order to build a small fire. Uncle took two small chips of chert out of his pouch, while Raven Wing shredded pine bark to make a nest. The sparks from the chert fell onto the pine bark, which smoldered, and then, as Raven Wing blew on it, a small flame shot up—not much of a fire, but Margaret guessed Topknot would never have allowed even a small fire if he believed they were being pursued.

It was only the second day; help could not be expected or even hoped for before the fifth day, by which time at the relentless pace Topknot set, Margaret figured they would be nearly one hundred miles from the Greenbrier Settlement, more if their horses were fed and watered adequately. She wondered at their leader's decision to press on regardless, knowing the Indians were famous for caring for their horses.

Exhausted, she sat down on a log and Agatha came and sat beside her. For a while they sat in silence. Then Margaret smoothed her sister's hair and tied her bonnet back on. She dabbed her fingers in her mouth, then tried to rub the marks of mud and tears off her sister's round cheeks. Agatha was mumbling something, Margaret guessed a prayer.

"Where is Pilgrim now?" she asked to divert her.

Agatha gathered herself. "He encounters Obstinate and attempts to persuade him to go along."

Margaret took up the role of Obstinate, which she had always enjoyed when they read the "Progress" beside the fire. "'What are the things you seek, seeing as you leave all the world to find them?'"

"I seek an inheritance incorruptible," Agatha recited, straightening up and strengthening her voice until it reached the Indians lounging on the other side of the fire. "It is laid up in heaven—"

A yell from the woods stopped her. The two brothers stepped out of the trees, a young deer slung by its legs from the pole they carried between them.

Uncle stepped forward and cut the thongs that bound the deer to the pole. It fell heavily. This, Margaret surmised, was his job— too old to hunt or fight but still useful as a butcher. Crouching over the deer, with a single slash he slit it from throat to waste hole, then peeled the hide back. He gutted it, laying the steaming entrails on a stone. The deer twitched, responding with a jerk as he sawed off fore and back quarters and carved the loin meat into thick slabs. Topknot took the liver and heart. Uncle hurled the rest of the entrails into the woods for the wolves and vultures.

Now Raven Wing, who'd been whittling sharp points on sticks, stepped forward to spear a slab of meat. He handed the other sticks around, and the party took to roasting their spears of meat over the dying flames. Margaret seized one slab to roast for Agatha. She had no appetite and gagged at the smell of the roasting meat, so lean no fat dripped onto the coals.

When her piece of meat was cooked, she helped Agatha tear it into bits that she crammed into her mouth. So dainty before with her handkerchief always at her lips, Agatha now ate like one of the savages, juice dripping down her chin.

After Brother One stamped out the remains of the fire, Topknot signaled with a motion of his hand that all should prepare to sleep. Margaret and Agatha had lost their buffalo robes in the battle, and although they were surely in the packs the Indians had loaded onto their horses, Margaret knew there was no use asking. The robes would be set aside, valuable for trade.

She and Agatha were obliged to nest as best they could on a bare piece of ground some distance from the warriors. They pulled their skirts down to their feet; it was warm enough still to manage. The Indians wrapped themselves in their blankets before stretching out nearer to the fire.

Uncle came to the two women and with gestures ordered them to take off their boots. Agatha began to whimper as she untied her strings till Margaret helped, which calmed her. They handed their boots to Uncle, who retreated a few feet, then settled on a stump to keep guard, his flintlock across his knees.

Margaret lay on her back and offered Agatha her shoulder for a pillow. As soon as her sister was asleep, she eased herself away, stretching out a few feet closer to the trees. The deep quiet of the night recalled one of her chief private joys. She dropped into sleep as though falling down a deep well.

An hour later, she felt her dress snatched up and John's breeches pulled down. Before the man could pin her arms, she drove the thumb and forefinger of her right hand into his nostrils. She ground her nails into the thin crusted flesh while he struggled to break her grip, tossing his head like a wild horse and spreading his knees to clamp hers. He seized her hand to wrench it away from his nose, but Margaret was strong. She dug her nails in more deeply and raised her mouth and bit his chin to the bone.

He yelled. She tasted the first trickle of warm blood.

"Let me go, God damn you!" he howled. She recognized the voice. It was Girty.

She unclamped her fingers and then, before he could begin another foray, she drew up her knee and jammed it into the juncture of his breeches.

He rolled off her, cursing, and crawled away into the darkness, where she heard him cursing and moaning for some time.

Sitting up to be sure Girty was gone, Margaret saw Topknot watching. Briefly, she wondered why he had not stopped the assault, then understood. She was not his. She was her own. A look she didn't know how to read passed over Topknot's face. It might almost have been a smile.

CHAPTER FIVE

IN THE CHILL damp before dawn, the camp was stirring. Brother One and Uncle gathered the men's horses from their makeshift corral in the woods. Agatha was waiting as though expecting her horse to be brought to her until Margaret hissed and led the way to get Jenny and Star.

Bringing their horses in, Margaret gestured to Uncle to give them their boots. Extracting them from his pack, he threw them onto the ground. Hastily, Margaret and Agatha tied them on, then mounted.

Topknot was standing at some distance, scanning the trees as though, Margaret thought, he was looking for a sign. For the first time, she wished for a language to speak to him, to find out what he thought was about to happen. She had begun to sense that he did understand some English. Greatly daring, she leaned down from her horse and asked, "Do you see an enemy coming?"

He ignored her. She expected nothing else. Yet asking the question relieved her.

Then the men mounted. Girty was nowhere to be seen.

"I could fancy some pone," Agatha said, riding up alongside Margaret.

"Drink a little of your water, Sister, it will quell the hunger pangs." Agatha screwed the top off her canteen and drank.

They were riding in the middle of the party. Topknot was leading, then Uncle, with Brother One and Brother Two following at the end. The little troop passed quickly through the morning woods. The rising sun shone on pale patches on the trail, well-worn and clear of stones.

A break in the trees showed a large river, glittering in the sunlight. Sand bars created eddies near the bank; out in the middle, the current ran fierce and strong, carrying a large tree, its branches raised to the sky.

At a word from Topknot, Brother One and Uncle skidded their horses down the bank and splashed into the water, sliding at the same time out of their saddles and seizing their horses' tails. Almost at once the horses lost their footing and began to thrash crosswise to the current, their riders yelling and hanging on. Brother Two plunged his horses in next and all three were soon in the middle of the river.

"Surely we will not be expected—" Agatha began.

"Hush." Margaret was watching Topknot haul a canoe out of the bushes. The canoe was narrow and Margaret feared for their lives if it should tip. She had never been taught to swim at the Greenbrier. Still, at a gesture from Topknot, she dismounted and stripped off her saddle and bridle. Agatha did the same. Topknot loaded their gear into the middle of the canoe and then beckoned them to climb in.

They climbed in without mishap. Then Topknot stepped in lightly and shoved off, taking up the paddle.

In the current, the canoe bucked and lunged. Topknot righted it and began to paddle at a slight angle, heading toward the far shore. The three horses floundered into the water and followed.

Margaret dared finally to loosen her hands from the sides of the canoe. She looked around. The other Indians were already on the far shore, their horses shaking off sheets of water.

She looked at Agatha. She was trailing her hand in the water as though they were on a holiday picnic and smiling at Topknot's back.

Margaret surmised that Agatha was going to use her old ways as though their captors were white men. Margaret did not count the Indians as men but as instruments of destiny only. Girty, although a monster, was a man because he was white. Yet Topknot's hands on the paddle, she saw, were hardly darker than her own. What strange mixture had gone into his creation!

Their canoe was approaching the bank. Margaret began to piece a map in her mind of the route they had traveled and realized what river they were crossing.

The Ohio.

The name called up no sweet associations as did the Shenandoah. She had never seen either river, but she knew the song and hummed it to herself for comfort: *Oh Shenandoah, I long to see you* . . . She felt her lips begin to quiver.

Agatha looked at her sharply. "Sister!"

"That old song—" She stopped.

Topknot was back-paddling hard to reach the bank.

"Pray for our deliverance," Agatha said. "Pray ceaselessly."

"Never," Margaret croaked, smearing her tears away with the back of one hand.

"Why, Sister—"

"Not since Father died. If He would do that—"

"The ways of the Lord are inscrutable," Agatha parroted.

"Then he's no lord of mine."

Brother One was wading into the water to catch the canoe as

Topknot brought it close to shore.

"Blasphemy," Agatha said softly, as though she was thinking it over. "You increase our peril."

"I'd as soon pray to that savage," Margaret said as Brother One seized the prow.

"Never!" Agatha cried.

"Step out, Sister—but carefully—"

"You first," Agatha said.

Crouching, Margaret maneuvered one foot over the edge and stepped down into the shallow water as the canoe swayed violently. Water rose to her knees. Then she held out her hand to Agatha, who stepped out daintily. Topknot had already climbed out of the canoe, turning his back on the two women and hurrying up the bank. Margaret dragged the canoe up the shore.

Agatha was still chewing the topic. "What foolishness to go out hunting in that blizzard! Everyone told him not to go."

"We were starving," Margaret said abruptly. "Father was desperate to feed us."

"And froze instead in a snow bank."

"Yet you believe in God . . ." As she spoke, Margaret was crawling up the steep bank on hands and knees. Then she stood, shaking out her wet skirts. Brother One was making a fire for the warriors to dry themselves, but she knew she would not be welcome at the blaze.

Quickly, she unfastened her waistband and stepped out of her soaked skirts. John's breeches were wet as well, but they would dry, exposed to the sun. Agatha made a small noise of objection, but Margaret paid her no mind. She threw her skirt down on the river bank and left it.

"You are indecent," Agatha said. She did not remove her own soaked garment.

Margaret did not bother to answer.

They found their gear in the pile on the shore and began to saddle and bridle their horses. Jenny was restive from the river and took some gentling before Margaret could cinch her girth.

Further up the bank, the Indians seemed to be conferring. Brother One was asserting something, Margaret thought, and Topknot was calmly disagreeing. Then Brother One turned and stared at the two women, a glare that Margaret understood too well. They were a hindrance, requiring the canoe to cross the river and then slow to saddle.

"Quick, Agatha," she said. "Brother One is saying we are delaying them."

Agatha stood gaping by Star.

Uncle came sliding down the bank, scowling. He grabbed Agatha by the arm and tossed her away like a dry weed.

Margaret helped her to scramble up. For the first time, her sister did not complain, and Margaret wondered if she was grateful to be spared a more serious punishment. They ran to their horses and mounted. The Indians were already riding into the trees.

Margaret looked back. Now the great river lay between them and deliverance. She felt a kind of clearing as though she had suffered a spell of dizziness that now had passed. She looked down at Jenny's neck and laid her hand along her mane. Brave little mare, pacing on steadily by the river, although unfed and terrified. When a green branch crossed their trail, Jenny snatched a few leaves.

As they rode on, Margaret felt a new wetness in her stained and wrinkled shirt waist. Her right breast was leaking its useless milk.

She kicked Jenny and urged Agatha on. They had fallen behind.

She heard her sister scream as her horse jolted forward, whipped from behind by Brother One. Mercifully, this time she did not fall. Margaret goaded Jenny into a trot, and the two women finally regained the rest of the party.

They rode for many hours on the west side of the river, through tall reed thickets that switched their faces, moving out at a trot as a cleared space, almost a pasture, opened in front of them.

Margaret groaned, bouncing on her chaffed thighs. The coarse leather of John's breeches ground against her. Yet she must keep up, must keep hissing at Agatha to hurry.

At the edge of the clearing they slowed, passing into woods from the riverside thickets: black walnut, hickory nut, and chestnut.

Her shirt waist was now soaked on both sides. Two days since her baby was murdered, yet her breasts were still dripping miserable drops of milk.

At a shout from Topknot, they halted. He pointed at Margaret with a sideways twist of his pursed mouth she had seen before: an order, wordless but clear. She opened her saddlebag and began to hand out her jerky, but she was not quick enough. Raven Wing snatched her saddlebag from its binding and poured the jerky out on the ground where all went for it.

She watched Topknot's hands sorting through the jerky. She thought, *You held my baby's feet in those hands. You held them long enough to feel her fine, firm flesh. Then you took a fresh hold and bashed her head against a tree.*

A beech, I think.

She saw her baby's face in that moment, mouth open in a wail. *Only a moment of terror before you flung her. If there is a God, I would thank him for that. And for her being nameless, not expected to live.*

Yes, it was a beech. There are many of them in the woods at home. Her little body like an empty sack dropped at the root of that tree. A beech.

And we rode on.

She knew they would ask her later—if she ever saw the Greenbrier Settlement again—why she hadn't snatched her baby from the Indian, bowing her head for the tomahawk. She would tell them that with her gone they would still have slaughtered her baby and probably Agatha as well, removing all impediments to their flight.

But truly there had been no time for such calculations.

The other answer, the answer she would never give them, was that she had wanted to live.

CHAPTER SIX

T HEY RODE NORTH all the next day.
Toward noon it began to rain, a cold rain, falling in sheets. The thick gray sky dropped down heavily over the woods where many of the trees were shedding their leaves, not in the colors of the Greenbrier Settlement but in dull browns and grays.

The rain soaked the saddle in front of Margaret where the baby had ridden and began to seep through her breeches. She shivered. Agatha, riding behind her, gasped, then sobbed. "I'm so cold!"

"Hush, Sister." Margaret glanced back. Agatha's fair face was pinched and pale under the lid of her bonnet. "Drink a little more of your water," Margaret told her.

"Gone!" Agatha wailed. She gestured avidly toward Margaret's canteen. "Better to give than to receive!"

Margaret passed her canteen and Agatha drank greedily. When she handed the canteen back, there were only a few drops left. But they were in well-watered country now and Margaret knew she would be able to fill her canteen whenever Topknot decided to stop. When that would happen was not clear.

Again, the two women were dropping behind. Uncle, who had moved in front of them earlier was disappearing among the trees ahead. The brothers, who had been riding behind them, had darted off in the woods, probably to track a deer.

Wildly, Margaret thought of turning and fleeing. But Star would never outrun the Indians' horses and she could not leave Agatha behind.

A whoop up ahead and Uncle came galloping back, his face clenched in a scowl. He slashed Agatha's horse with his whip. Star lurched forward, colliding with Jenny, who broke into a canter. Jolting, sliding, the two women rode ahead, while Uncle, behind them, went on lashing their horses. A branch struck Margaret in the face as she heard Agatha scream, "I'm falling!"

But she did not fall, and by the time they reached the rest of the party, she had stopped crying. Her lips were moving, Margaret supposed in prayer. She drew up beside her: "Speak, Sister."

Uncle was still herding them along, but Agatha managed to quote, "He therefore who went before (Vain-Confidence by name), not seeing the way before him fell into a deep pit."

Margaret found herself smiling, the smile cracking her stiff lips. "They are not likely to let either of us go before," she said. As Agatha began again to sniffle, she added, "Courage, Sister!" then wondered how often she would say it before the words ran dry. A maple dropped a brown leaf on her arm. Looking down, she saw that her shirtwaist had finally dried to stiffness. A sob seized her by the throat but she thrust it down.

In the afternoon, they passed out of the woods onto a rolling, grassy plain, where Margaret almost expected to see cattle grazing. She remembered a phrase Daniel Boone had recited when he stopped at their cabin door: "Kentucky, Land of Milk and Honey."

But they were too far north and west to be in that country, and after the bloody sevens, those years that had sent so many settlers fleeing back from the violence, she wondered how many still longed for that promised land. And now here she was, a husband-less, childless woman alone with savages, in charge willy-nilly of her sister.

They crossed a creek clattering over stones. Margaret guessed from the angle of the sun that it was near four o'clock. Shortly, Topknot called a halt. She knew from the earlier hour and the big fire the brothers built that they no longer feared pursuit. They had come too far, and the big river lay between. She pressed down a pang of panic.

Dismounting, she helped Agatha slide down from her horse. Immediately Agatha broke free and ran to the creek. Lying on her belly, she lapped the water like a dog.

The Indians dismounted and began to fill their canteens. The horses gathered at the edge of the water, sucking it up.

Raven Wing finished filling his canteen and came up the bank to where Margaret was standing. He was tall, dark-complected, with a large head and a single eagle feather stuck in his topknot.

He held out his right hand.

Astonished, Margaret reached to meet his hand.

He struck her to the ground.

Time passed before Margaret regained consciousness, time enough for the two brothers to return with a pair of rabbits. Half dazed by the blow, Margaret stood up. The ways of these savages would always be unpredictable. Her people's gesture of friendship, the extended right hand, had some other meaning, indecipher-able here. Anger or resentment were useless. She began to accept that she did not understand and perhaps would never understand. Ignorance put her and Agatha at greater risk. She decided to watch the Shawnee more closely and to learn.

Now she watched Brother One skin and gut the rabbits, noting his quickness with his knife. He split the carcasses into four dripping pieces, then suspended them on forked sticks over the fire. Rain dripped into the fire, threatening to put it out, but it flared up again as the rabbit juices hit.

Margaret slid down the bank to fill her canteen. Coming back up, she smelled the rich savor of roasting rabbit and knew she would have to eat. What a miserable sight they all looked, their clothes dark with rain as they crouched over the fire.

When the meat was only half done, Uncle tossed her part of a leg. She chewed the stringy ligaments off and set her teeth into a pocket of thigh flesh, succulent, nearly raw. Gagging, she choked it down, her hunger more powerful than her disgust. Agatha, crouched in the dirt, was tearing meat off a leg with her teeth. A good sign, Margaret thought. There was no use for dainty ways here.

"I thought you'd surely fall and break a bone when Raven Wing whipped Star," she said between bites.

"Never!" Agatha said disdainfully. "Raven Wing? What kind of a name?"

"I thought it best to give them all names."

Agatha huffed. "You have allowed your imagination to run away with you," she said crossly. "I think it would be to your benefit to leave them as they are, nameless savages with whom we must always contend!" At her tone, Margaret felt a great relief. She no longer needed to repeat, "Courage!" The lesson was learned before the words dried up.

She said soothingly, "Thank you for your correction. I see now why you are such a good wife to Alan. He also at times lets his imagination off the leash." She was remembering his owl hoots and wolf howls that had brought trouble down upon them.

"Alan is dead." Agatha tore off another piece of meat. "I saw him laid out on the trail with the scalping knife doing its unholy work."

In the three days since the attack, Margaret thought, Agatha had absorbed the sight, chewing, swallowing, and digesting it like a tough bit of meat.

Margaret said, "At least the knife did not do its work on John—"

Agatha interrupted, "My man stayed to fight. They tomahawked him and took his scalp. It will go to Detroit, to the scalp buyer. It will fetch a good price. He had—" her voice faltered—"beautiful fair hair. But your John," she added silkily, "ran away."

Margaret flared. "He was shot in the side, bleeding—I saw him—running as best he could to give the alarm!"

"Do you think he died on the way?" Agatha asked solicitously.

"No! He was determined to make it to the fort"—but even as she said it, she knew it could not be so; John was already stumbling as she watched him. She remembered how the Indians had stared at him, amazed that he had even been able to get up off the ground.

"Then praise God!" Agatha said, raising her face to the rain.

Margaret said nothing. Hope was too precious to waste on words.

Finally, the rain stopped. At a slight rise of ground, they made ready for the night. It passed slowly for Margaret in a half sleep of pain. She had struck a rock with her shoulder when Raven Wing felled her and the ache took over her mind and darkened her seeing.

When the Indians roused in the gray dawn, Margaret saw Agatha's face as she sat up; she looked parched, pale, and drawn. The rabbit, Margaret guessed, had gone down badly. Agatha, with a pitiful gesture, pointed to her skirt, and Margaret saw it was heavily stained and smelled the stench.

"You should have gone to the woods!"

"That old Indian (it was Uncle she meant) never lets us rise at night, you know that—and I have no boots."

Margaret rose quickly and went to Topknot, who was packing his saddlebags. She had noticed the day before that he seemed to understand a few words of English. He had looked sharply at the two women when they were disputing about John's escape.

"Ill," Margaret announced, pointing at Agatha. "Water!"

Topknot seemed to grasp the situation. He pointed toward the creek and said a word Margaret understood as *go*. She repeated the crude sound until she had learned it. Someday that *go* might mean freedom.

She helped Agatha down to the creek. Partly shielded by the trees, she stripped off her skirt and petticoat, all heavily stained and stinking, and plunged them in the cold water. She watched the current carry the defilement away.

Shivering on the bank, Agatha was trying to cover herself with her hands.

"Nobody is looking at you," Margaret said. The Indians were busy breaking camp. It seemed an aspect of the Shawnees' modesty that they took no interest in naked white women.

Margaret wrung out the garments and knotted them into a bundle. Agatha would catch her death if she wore them wet, and there was no chance the Indians would allow time to dry the things in the sun.

Leaving her sister huddled by the creek, Margaret went back to camp. In the bustle of leaving, she managed to snatch a blanket.

As she turned with it back to the creek, she felt Topknot's eyes, but he did not stop her.

At the creek, Agatha was cleaning herself with handfuls of wet leaves, then using more leaves to dry. Margaret noticed with dismay how childlike her naked body appeared, white, fleshless, the underlying bones rising through the parchment skin. Agatha had never been well-fleshed, but four days with only a bit of jerky and rejected wild rabbit had reduced her even further.

She wrapped the blanket around Agatha's shoulders and knotted it securely.

"But how will I mount?" the girl cried.

"As best you can," Margaret said stoutly. She would not waste her pity on such trifles. Still, when Agatha went to climb on Star, Margaret stood behind her, shielding her, then, once she was mounted, helped her spread the blanket over her knees. She undid the bundle of wet clothes and spread them on Star's rump, where they would dry in time.

Then they were off, following the one word—*Go!*—from Topknot.

CHAPTER SEVEN

BY AFTERNOON they were passing through another swath of fine country, rolling pastures rich with lush grass. Slackening their pace, the Shawnee allowed the horses to browse along the trail.

At noon, Topknot called a halt. Agatha led Star out into the grass and Margaret followed with Jenny. As the horses began to graze, the two sisters squatted nearby, watching them.

Margaret said, "John dreamed of this kind of pasturage. He might have found it in Kentucky. First frost will kill it all. But next spring I suppose more of the same. This land is not worn out here, there is no one to crop it."

Agatha was not attending, holding her belly with both hands and groaning. She crawled behind a tree and noisily did her business. Margaret went to her. "I have help here." She pulled the little pouch from its string around her neck, poured a few pinches of her mother's dried and crumbled blackberry leaves into her palm, then moistened it from her canteen. "Swallow!" Agatha gagged it down.

Then Topknot shouted and the sisters hastily gathered their horses and mounted, Margaret boosting Agatha into her saddle. She was soon listing sideways.

Margaret reined in Jenny and when Brother One galloped up, whip raised, she stopped him with her right hand spread wide. So there was a way, at least at that moment. She supported Agatha with her arm, preventing her from sliding.

Topknot came cantering back. She told him, "Sick!"—another word she thought he might understand, then instantly regretted it. The word might announce Agatha's end. She tightened her hold on her sister. They would go down together.

Topknot glared at the two women, then shouted something to Raven Wing, waiting at the front of the line. Raven Wing cantered back, drawing a length of rope from his saddlebag, which he tossed to Topknot. Separating Margaret from Agatha as easily as warm butter is separated with a cold knife, he bent Agatha forward and lashed her shoulders to her horse's neck, her arms dangling. The blanket covering her began to slide, and Margaret reached to tuck it in around her. Then, cantering to the front of the line, Topknot said the word that impelled them all forward: "Go!"

Agatha stayed bound all that afternoon. Riding close beside her, Margaret whispered encouragement, but her sister seemed to have fainted and did not respond. By good luck, their pace was slow as they were breaking trail through a thick stand of cane, the tops towering several feet overhead. The horses were lunging at the cane, breaking off sections and chomping them loudly.

At dusk Agatha finally roused herself and tried to break loose from her bonds, but Margaret ordered her to stay still and her sister obeyed. After a while she fell asleep, her bound body rocking to Star's pacing.

It was almost dark when Topknot called a halt in a bare patch of ground near a creek. The brothers were dismissed to hunt, and Uncle made a small fire in a circle of stones. Then he took a quantity of parched corn out of his pouch, looking at the sisters.

Margaret was untying Agatha, who slid to the ground, then stood up brightly. Her nap and the potion had restored her; there were patches of pink in her cheeks. She hitched up her blanket as Uncle seized her left arm, at the same time seizing Margaret's right elbow. He began to pull them up the slope.

Agatha resisted but when Margaret hissed, she went along. Margaret had brought her sister's clothes, which had dried on her horse's rump and now she hastily dressed her, Uncle turning away from the sight.

At the top of the rise, Uncle found a large flat stone. He pushed the two women to their knees beside it. Then he tossed handfuls of parched corn onto the stone, fetched two smaller stones, and pressed them into the women's hands.

"This is good news, Sister," Margaret told Agatha. "He is setting us to a task."

Margaret began at once to pound kernels with her stone. Agatha followed suit. Uncle continued to add corn. They pounded until the sun set and the first star winked out, ending with two piles of corn almost as fine as sand.

Uncle gathered the ground corn into his pouch and then, pushing the two women ahead of him, returned to the camp by the creek.

The brothers came back empty-handed, explaining their failure to find game with large gestures. Topknot frowned with displeasure. Margaret guessed that they were within a few miles of a settler's cabin or even a fort whose hunters had cleared the neighborhood of all prey. Again, she thought of escaping, but the thought had grown dim and faraway.

Topknot picked up a gourd dipper from the goods thrown down beside the fire and thrust it at Brother One, then waved him toward the creek. He hurried to fill the gourd, then brought it to Uncle, who emptied the water into his pouch of ground corn. Uncle gestured at the two women to kneel, then placed the pouch on the ground in front of them. At once, Margaret began to knead the pounded corn into the water, Agatha imitating her, their fingers brushing. They kneaded until the mixture resembled a thin gruel.

Meanwhile, Raven Wing, directed by Topknot, kicked dirt over the fire. Margaret guessed they could not risk smoke that night. The brothers, out hunting, must have seen something that had caused alarm, perhaps even the smoke from a settler's chimney. A lone cabin would have been easy pickings, but a fort, had they seen one, promised too great a danger.

Gathering around Uncle's pouch, they all began to dip in their fingers, spooning the gruel into their mouths. Agatha managed to scoop as much as the greediest Indian, forging her way through a forest of elbows. Margaret was relieved. Her sister would be able to go on in the morning.

Margaret was close to the Shawnee as they ate, and again she caught their strange smoky smell. Their fingers were meeting in the gruel, brushing, then pulling apart. She remembered eating with her brothers and sisters from her mother's pot of chicken stew. Their fingers had brushed in the same way, among the pieces of chicken.

She thought, *We are all the same: hungry, nearly starving.*

Later, the gruel gone, they were settling down for the night when an owl hooted from the cane brake. Immediately the Indians rose, seized their flintlocks, and began to load.

Girty stepped out of the cane brake, leading his horse. "Now don't you go to murdering your one true friend," he said to the warriors.

The Indians lowered their guns, and Topknot greeted Girty. The two men spoke rapidly. Margaret guessed that Girty brought news of a settlement nearby. They were predicting, planning. It seemed that Girty acted as a kind of scout, trusted as a longtime friend.

Then Girty hobbled his horse with the others hidden in the cane brake and made his way to Margaret. She stood staring at him, her fists clenched by her sides. He came so close she could see the marks of her teeth on his chin.

"Stand back," she said, thrusting her fists against his shoulders.

He stood still. "No need to fear, Missy. I like 'em with a little more meat on their bones."

She sneered her disgust.

"They'll make squaws of the both of you," he told her.

Agatha, overhearing, began to protest.

"Why would they want to do that?" Margaret asked evenly, dropping her fists. "We are the daughters of their enemies."

"Smallpox last winter took a lot of their squaws. A poor crop of babies last spring."

Agatha was storming. "We are white!"

Girty turned on her. "Half breed better than no breed. I'll thank you to stop your yelling."

"How do you know these Shawnee?" Margaret asked, knowing Girty's aid might come in handy.

"Long story, Missy. Eighteen years ago when we was at Fort Granville on the Juniata River, a war party burned the fort to the ground. They tortured my stepfather, John Turner, to death, and taken the rest of us captives. My brother went to the Senecas, and the rest of us boys got adopted by the Shawnee. When the treaty was signed at Fort Pitt, all the boys was turned loose. The others had a bellyful and went back East, but I stayed and served as interpreter. I reported to Alexander McKee."

"Then surely you will help us," Margaret said, "as you are presenting yourself as the Shawnee's friend. Word of the way we are treated here will get back to Virginia."

Girty laughed. "Maybe and maybe not, Missy," he said, then jumped on his horse and rode off into the woods.

Standing nearby, Topknot had been listening to the exchange. Margaret turned to him, spreading her hands to show her confusion. "Friend?" she asked, guessing this was a word Topknot knew.

He turned away without answering.

CHAPTER EIGHT

NEXT MORNING, Margaret was waked before dawn by the thump of two bodies falling. Two Shawnee were fighting, now up and swinging, now down and rolling in the dirt.

Grappling, they rolled even closer, and she saw it was the youths she thought of as Brother One and Raven Wing.

She shrank back. She could smell their sweat, strong and sweet. She wanted to call out to Topknot, but something held her back. Brother One was bleeding copiously from his nose. And yet he was smiling. Was this some game of skill?

Then she saw Topknot standing over the two writhing bodies. They must have sensed his presence for they separated suddenly, rolling apart, panting. Brother One was swiping the blood from his nose.

Topknot said a word and swept his arm toward the woods. The two fighters scrambled up and started off at once.

Topknot looked at Margaret, huddled in her blanket.

"No fear," he said.

Now there were two more words in English he knew and probably, Margaret thought, a great many more as well.

"I wasn't frightened," she said, thinking he meant the fight. "Was it a game?"

Clearly not understanding, Topknot gestured toward Girty who stood at the edge of the encampment, saddling his horse.

"No squaw," Topknot said.

He had overheard and understood Girty's threat.

"Thank you," Margaret said. She had no other words for her relief.

Now Agatha was sitting up, hastily gathering her blanket around her.

"Are you recovered, Sister?" Margaret asked.

Agatha nodded and smiled, her smile reminding Margaret of the Greenbrier. No one smiled here.

Her smile vanished. "What am I to eat?" she wailed.

"Think of the horses," Margaret said. "They are starving, too."

Agatha was not to be quieted. "They browse! I cannot eat grass! I shall chew bark!"

Margaret had held back some of her gruel the night before. She went to fetch it now. It had hardened considerably in the leather pouch, but she broke it into small chunks and fed it to Agatha, reserving some for herself. Agatha made a face at the dried gruel, but she choked it down. Margaret ate a few pieces, washing them down with water from her canteen.

A whoop from the woods startled them. Brother One and Raven Wing broke out of the trees, their arms filled with dried corncobs. Margaret thought they must have raided a settler's barn for corn left after the last harvest, little enough, but a feast for the starving horses. She darted forward and snatched four cobs for Jenny and Star; still hobbled, they stood among the trees, their ears alertly pricked. She fed them the cobs one at a time.

The Indians were already mounted when she came back. Hastily, the two women saddled and clambered onto their horses. The party started off single file, Topknot and Raven Wing in the lead, Brother One and Uncle behind.

Late in the afternoon, Topknot halted on a prow of land and Margaret saw the great river glittering in the distance. They had been riding northwest for five days, she calculated, about a mile from the western bank. They had gone at least two hundred miles from their capture.

Topknot gestured to the party to dismount. Agatha slid down, groaning. Her skirt and petticoat did not protect her legs from chafing against the stirrup leathers. Margaret's legs fared better in John's stout breeches.

Over the trees, Margaret saw a sickle moon rising with its attendant star, glowing as the air grew chill. She remembered her mother calling the new moon a slipper moon, although it seemed unlikely Nancy had ever worn slippers. But after all, Margaret thought as she hobbled Jenny, her mother had had a life in Pittsburgh before she married. Perhaps there had been slippers there. More and more it seemed that everything Margaret thought she knew was becoming doubtful, as though the past itself, or what she had thought was the past, was shifted by the present. Wryly, she thought that was what was meant by education gained through travel.

As she settled herself for the night in the notch between two big tree roots, Margaret realized that she was becoming used to life on the trail. Never comfortable (she was beginning to feel the chill even now), never out of danger, but accommodating herself to both. John's death and her infant's destruction were beginning to sink away into a life she could barely remember.

Five days. Do lives mean so little?

Raven Wing was building a big fire when she woke the next morning. Margaret knew this meant they were now so far from cabin or fort there was no chance of detection.

The flames were licking up from the logs, and Margaret stretched out her hands, relishing the warmth. Then she bethought herself of her housewife. She fetched her saddlebag and took out the little almanack with her stoppered vial of pokeberry ink and chicken feather quill. Opening the almanack at random, she laid her finger on a phrase: "After crosses and losses, men grow humble and wise." She dipped her quill in the ink and wrote small letters in the space beneath Mr. Franklin's words: "I am growing accustomed."

Was it the methodical way they were proceeding, the neat pattern of days, each like the last, that made the life at home seem random, almost disordered? Margaret's life before had seemed governed by chance, even when John was ordering her about. She hadn't always obeyed, and then chance had taken over. And in the Greenbrier there had always been much arguing when a man took it upon himself to issue an order. Fetch firewood, fetch water— even when the need was obvious, the order was obeyed, slowly and with much grumbling.

No one grumbled here, although life was not easy and Topknot's few orders were obeyed swiftly.

She remembered Mr. Franklin's words in the little old book: "Savages we call them, because their manners differ from ours, which we think the Perfection of Civility; they think the same of theirs."

Whatever the reason, she was growing accustomed.

She stoppered her vial after writing the one sentence and put her things away.

CHAPTER NINE

IN THE DIMNESS before dawn, Raven Wing had brought down a small brown bear with a single shot. He had found the beast in another abandoned cornfield by the edge of the river Margaret had thought was the Kanawha.

Girty had corrected her: "We're a long way from the Kanawha, Girl. That over there's the Ohio."

"So Topknot never did plan on going down to Kentucky," Margaret said.

"Not in the leastest. Their place is northwesterly from here."

"Is that where we're heading?"

Girty did not answer. He went to help butcher the bear.

Agatha rode up beside her. "What's that the ruffian was saying?"

"Ruffian maybe, but useful. Says that river down there's not the Kanawha. It's the Ohio."

"Why do you converse with him?" Agatha asked.

"He knows things," Margaret said.

The Shawnee were all occupied now with the carcass of the bear, butchering and building a fire for roasting. When the butchering was completed, sections of the bear were roasted over the fire and the company ate better than they had since the deer.

Afterward Margaret sat on a fallen limb and began to mend a tear in her shirt sleeve where the cloth had caught on a stubborn thorn. She'd hidden her sewing kit in her housewife; it seemed a novelty to the Indians, and Uncle stood watching as she steadily stitched. He said something to Topknot, who came to watch as well.

Their attention caused Margaret to wonder if they took her needlework as a form of magic. Their belts were beautifully beaded in red and blue, but that work was of a different order from her mending. She had noticed that their shirts were often torn at the sleeve or underarm, and she began to imagine that her mending might be useful to them once they had arrived at their village.

Having accepted one bit of information from Girty, she decided to try for another. Catching his eye—he was often watching her— she asked, "How many more days on the trail?"

"By my calculations, three, if we keep up a steady pace and the weather conspires to aid us," he told her.

Both seemed likely. This was the first day they had stopped for more than a brief night of sleeping, and late September was usually a time of settled fair weather although the cold was steadily increasing.

"Three days!" Agatha, overhearing, exclaimed. "And then in the name of God, where?"

"Shawnee Old Town, Chillicothe, they call it, if it is still standing," Simon said, "and a warm welcome you'll be receiving there."

Both women had heard tales of the Indians' warm welcome. Agatha clutched Margaret's arm. "He means the gauntlet!"

"We've run worse," Margaret reassured her, although what she meant was childbirth, which her sister had not yet undergone. But there were other pains of womanhood they had both endured, uncomplaining. It could not be discussed openly in the Greenbrier, but young wives often referred at the washing kettles or in the fields to the horrors of their wedding nights.

She decided to assay Simon once again. "Is this the Wilderness Trail we're traveling?"

Before he could answer, Topknot spoke a word across the fire that stopped him. But later when they were saddling, Simon told her, "The Wilderness Trail is the Cumberland Gap way, south of us now by many miles. The Long Knives call this the Warriors' Trace. They never come here. Shawnee territory!"

Margaret did not need to ask if the Long Knives—the Virginians—were less likely to pursue them on the Path. This was Shawnee country, most dangerous to the settlers.

"They will fight to the death for this last scrap of their territory," Simon told her.

Soon they turned west and rode all afternoon along a river Margaret heard the Shawnee call the Scioto. The trail was rocky here but Agatha, strengthened by the bear meat, jolted along singing, *Oh the briary bush, the briary bush that pricks my heart so sore,* till Topknot put an end to it with a shout.

Perhaps that meant, Margaret thought, even while she knew her hope was vain, that there was still a chance they were being followed. Surely one of their neighbors in the Greenbrier was brave enough to essay the Warriors' Trace and to call on the courage of other men to join him.

She assembled these rescuers in her imagination: her husband, John, of course, his terrible wound miraculously healed, his nephew Nathan, a big tall lad who had spent most of his eighteen years hunting in the woods, Agatha's older brother, Moses, also a keen hunter and a giant of a man, and surely a few more. It was common duty for men from the settlement to pursue those taken by Indians, although to her recollection they were seldom successful. She remembered that one party a few years back had returned empty-handed because the Shawnee captive, Will Henderson's wife, Sarah, had refused to return. Her Indian captor, who had made her a part of his family, turned down all offers of ransom. Will had cursed Sarah to her face for her disloyalty and galloped away with the other men, leaving her to her Indian family, where she still remained.

Margaret found the tale curiously thrilling. She imagined Sarah's face, set against her husband's attempts at persuasion and then set against his cursing. Sarah had been one of the many wives at the Greenbrier whose character seemed planed by hard work; physically nothing had distinguished her from the others. Now, in Margaret's imagining, her face looked changed, as though each of her features was more clearly marked. It was a strange thought, one she could not have anticipated.

That afternoon Margaret felt her spirits rise, strengthened to a degree by the bear meat. The horses had been allowed to graze while their masters ate; once she mounted, Margaret could feel Jenny's filled belly between her legs. And Agatha was well and even cheerful. It seemed possible they would reach Chillicothe before another evil overtook them—but also before a rescue party picked up their trail. Margaret suspected that her neighbors and relatives would not dare approach the Shawnee village.

She wondered why she had never heard in the Greenbrier of the Warriors' Trace. The talk had always been of the Wilderness Trail and the excitement of the first look over the mountains at Cumberland Gap. That trail led to the fertile grasslands of Kentucky and D. Boone's fort, the most secure, everyone said, of any fort west of the Appalachians.

Simon Girty was again at hand, riding at her side. She said, "I heard Boone's fort survived a frightful eleven-day siege by the Shawnee."

Simon chuckled. "There was a reason for that, Missy. Boone was captured first, but he escaped their camp and made it back to the fort to bring the warning, so cool-headed he stopped along the way to measure out and mark a tract for his future possession."

"That would surprise no one who knew Boone," Margaret said. "But everyone in the Greenbrier wondered when they heard the young women went out the gates and let down their hair."

"As the Shawnee warriors requested. The braves called out, 'Pretty squaws! Pretty squaws!'"

Pretty squaws. Margaret did not find that fitting. "In any event, although the settlers were sorely wasted, the fort held."

"For eleven days till the warriors withdrew, it was said because of the rain, but the Shawnee take no account of weather."

They rode on after dark although the trail was nearly impossible to see. Agatha began to weep with exhaustion by the time the first stars appeared above the trees and the new moon, a little thickened, rose. Margaret tried to divert her. "Where are Christian and his friends now, Sister?"

At first Agatha did not respond but after Margaret repeated the question, she said in a tear-cracked voice, "They fell suddenly into a bog. The name of the bog was Despond. Here, they wallowed for a time, and Christian began to sink."

"Because of the burden on his back," Margaret reminded her.

Agatha went on in a stronger voice, "Truly, Christian said, I do not know where we are."

"We are traveling along the Scioto River," Margaret told her with assurance. "There are no bogs anywhere here about," and she was rewarded by Agatha's dim smile.

They rode on in silence, picking their way along the trail with Topknot and Raven Wing leading as usual and Brother One and Uncle bringing up the rear. The women rode in the middle of the company. Girty stayed nearby, sometimes disappearing into the woods.

Before the moon had set, Agatha began to moan again, undone by fatigue. Fearing that she would faint and fall from her saddle, Margaret kicked Jenny and rode to the front of the line, intending to persuade Topknot to halt. Without even turning to look at her, he shoved her back with his arm so forcefully she almost fell. As she grabbed Jenny's mane and regained her seat, the Shawnee filed past her without a look. Agatha, riding up, scolded her for her daring.

"Then compose yourself," Margaret told her, more harshly than she had intended. But the remonstrance seemed to do Agatha good; she rode on with no further ado. Margaret reined Jenny in behind Star, for the first time allowing her sister to take the lead.

It was closer to dawn than midnight when they finally stopped, with no time to build a fire or set up camp. Margaret and Agatha hobbled their horses. They slept that night on the bare ground with their heads on their saddles for the few hours Topknot allotted. The blankets were still packed in the saddlebags, but at least the weather was moderating a little. But as the moon set, a sharp breeze set in and the cold wakened them even before Topknot's shout.

They started off with only sips from their canteens for sustenance. Jenny and Star, again ravenous, craned to snatch leaves from the trees overarching the trail until Raven Wing struck them with his whip and they jolted forward.

All morning Simon Girty skirted the party before riding off toward the river.

"Why was our night so short?" Margaret asked him as he passed.

He grimaced. "Bad spirits there, no place to linger. Big fight. Cornstalk led the attack." Then he rode on.

Margaret reined in as Agatha rode up beside her. "Did you hear that?" Margaret asked.

Her sister nodded. "Uncle Tom took part in that foray. Lost his right arm—I heard the story. More than a day fighting the Indian war party and in the end hand to hand. We lost something upward of a dozen men before we forced the savages back across the river. They have good reason to fear this place."

"These Shawnee fought?"

"God knows. Them, or some like them."

"But we have murdered too," Margaret said. It was a thought some time forming. "Their chief who came to one of our forts under a flag of truce—"

"Cornstalk. Killed, his son, as well, and one other. A year ago this November. But you know, Sister, they had caused the death of many."

"But they carried the white flag!"

"I doubt much that the savages knew its meaning." Agatha was as always fiercely fixed on her opinion.

Margaret set herself to understanding why she had largely failed to notice the news Agatha had swallowed but could find no excuse except the mob of children in her mother's cabin. The noise never ceased from before dawn to darkest night and sometimes in the reaches of night as well: bawling, screeching, shouting, whining, weeping, laughing—some of the last as well—but mainly the crush and tumble of small half-naked bodies hurtling against each other in play or war, and all in one room. Their mother went about her chores without attending to her children, other than to give a slap here and there when the uproar proved unbearable, or turn them all out of the cabin. Even after she married, Margaret had spent most of her days in her mother's cabin, sensing her need for help although she knew better than to expect gratitude. She was merely doing her duty.

Margaret had tried to copy her but without much success. Small grubby hands were always pulling at her skirt or a child had swallowed a button halfway down and had to be saved from choking or Jacky, who had not yet mastered the control of his bowels, had squatted and made a mess in the corner. All of this and more filled her ears and eyes because she was the oldest girl: snatching at Lucy's hair to yank out a knot, buttoning the back of Sarah's dress, wiping the older boys' feet at the door before they tracked in mud—all this she did or it would not be done. And so her ears had been stopped to the news of the world whereas Agatha, youngest of only three children and without a child of her own, had room for all of it. The opinions of their neighbors, expressed as they read aloud from a shared newspaper, had penetrated Agatha as well, forming her fierce opinions.

Although often weeks old, the newspaper was read with avidity and its reports were repeated, sometimes with strange distortions and embellishments. In this way Margaret had heard of the great white general's near defeat far up north and his retreat across a half-frozen river before his triumphant capture of an entire British regiment. Much later she learned that this battle represented the downfall of the invaders, soon sent flying in their ships back across the ocean.

But that news had roused various opinions at the Greenbrier, some worrying that the colonists were now alone in the wilderness, others foretelling that the French or even the Spanish would come in to fill the vacuum.

CHAPTER TEN

THE AFTERNOON PASSED slowly. Margaret was beginning again to be very hungry. Her stomach cramped as it had during a winter two years before when a meager harvest and poor hunting had left the Greenbrier Settlement nearly starved. That had been good preparation for what she was now enduring. Hunger might become, she thought, almost an everyday thing.

Agatha, for once, did not complain. She had fallen into conversation with Simon Girty, who had circled back through the woods to join the party, a brace of wild turkey slung from his saddle. "More feathers than meat," he warned Margaret when he saw her looking at the birds hungrily. "But a morsel, maybe, for each of you after the warriors have eaten."

He went on talking to Agatha. Margaret craned to hear their conversation. She hoped it would be more bits and pieces about the war in the east—that might come in handy later.

But Girty's information was scanty. The English forces were still engaged, causing mayhem and destruction on the far eastern shore of the Atlantic Ocean. Closer at hand, a white general, George Clark, was organizing a big group of militia. Clark was a fierce warrior, and the Shawnee had learned to fear his military excursions. He was coming with his force up the Ohio.

That afternoon Topknot called for an earlier halt than usual, and Margaret noticed a sort of ease around the campfire she had not seen before. The Indians lounged and dozed. Even old Uncle was allowed off his perch for a while. The wild turkeys, when plucked, cleaned, and roasted, provided more than a mouthful for each of the party. She and Agatha ate last, as usual, but their portions were almost plentiful. After she had slowly chewed and swallowed hers the better to relish it, Margaret allowed herself to lean back on a log, for the first time. Except when asleep, she always sat upright. Nearby, Agatha was nearly sprawling.

Raven Wing was carving a new handle to replace one broken from his scalping knife—Margaret did not allow herself to imagine in what fearful encounter. Brother One was fletching his arrows, Uncle was carefully cleaning a cut on his heel and poulticing it with a pad of moss. Even Topknot, always alert to the point of springing, sat leaning against a tree trunk with his eyes closed.

When Simon Girty passed close by, Margaret beckoned to him. "We are all at ease tonight," she commented cautiously, then realized it was the first time she has spoken of them all as one. "Do they not know of the white general's approach?"

"I saw no reason to alarm them," Simon told her. "In any event, we will reach Old Chillicothe tomorrow, if it's still standing."

"Why, what would have become of it?" she asked.

"Long Knives already burned it twice," Girty said, then quickly moved on.

Aware of the approaching change in their situation, Margaret bethought herself of her journal to record their last evening on the trail. She rose to search through her saddlebag and noticed that Topknot had opened his eyes to watch her. Pulling out the little book, her vial of ink, and quill pen, she settled herself to write a few lines. "This day we were allowed to rest a little, our goal apparently being nearby." Then she stretched herself on the ground beside Agatha and fell asleep.

Uncle roused the sisters before dawn, shaking them roughly by their shoulders. They had perhaps overslept a little, Margaret thought. She wondered that oversleeping had been allowed, then reminded herself that she understood nothing of their captors' behavior. A sufferance she might call kindness dropped abruptly into brutality with no easily perceived cause.

They rode all day at a fast pace through beechwoods and bramble thickets. A dreary grayness clouded the afternoon, and presently it began to rain. Rain soaked through Margaret's breeches and soon she began to shiver as the cold afternoon closed in. She felt fatigue rising in sobs she choked back. Her legs scarcely had the strength to hold to Jenny, and her hands trembled on the wet reins. She turned to Agatha, sloped sideways on her saddle, and reached to comfort her. There would be no mercy for either of them if they fell.

"Courage, Sister, look at me," she said, feeling strengthened when Agatha lifted her head. Holding her upright with one arm, Margaret whispered urgently, "Remember Pilgrim!" then dug from memory the needed passage: "Do you see yonder shining light?"

Agatha answered feebly, "I think I do."

"Keep that light in your eye, Sister. According to Girty, we'll reach their town before nightfall—the reason for this haste."

"But what then?" Agatha asked.

Margaret had no answer. "Keep your eye on that light," she said, bringing all the strength she had left into her voice. Agatha managed to right herself and stay up without further assistance.

At sundown the Shawnee reined in and sent up a hallo, then fired their flintlocks into the air. Jenny, frightened, plunged and bucked, but Margaret managed to keep her seat. The Shawnee roared with laughter. Then they rode at breakneck speed down a bank and forded a stream.

She heard answering whoops and shouts as they galloped toward a cluster of long bark- covered houses, standing in a clearing around a space of bare earth. Smoke was rising from many fires. A crowd of Indians was running toward them, hooting and shouting with every appearance of jubilation.

Now Topknot gave forth a cry Margaret had not heard before. She guessed he was announcing their return with prisoners, plunder, and scalps. The welcoming crowd responded with strident hallos.

Margaret dismounted with the rest of the party and stood waiting, holding Jenny's reins, for whatever might now befall them. She kept Agatha and her horse within reach, determined to protect her to the end.

In front of them, a double line of Indians was assembling, each man, woman, and child armed with a stick or a club. The narrow passage between the two lines was the gauntlet she'd heard all captives were required to run.

She stepped forward with her head high. The only possible reprieve would come if she showed courage. Agatha was trembling at her side.

Topknot halted both women with his arm. It seemed that, strangely enough, some mercy had been extracted. Later she would learn the reason.

Immediately two young white boys were pushed forward and shoved violently into the entrance of the gauntlet. Sticks and clubs were raised, then blows rained down as they crouched and ran forward, shielding their heads. After one particularly vicious blow across his neck, the larger of the two boys turned on his assailant, snatched his club, and struck him smartly across the jaw. At that the crowd began to hoot and laugh, the double lines quickly dispersed, and the boys were led into a large house.

Margaret and Agatha, prodded forward, followed them.

This council house—msi-kah-miqui, as Margaret would learn to call it—was made from tall saplings, stripped of their bark and lashed together. The house was almost ninety feet in length, Margaret calculated, with a hide-covered door at either end and smoke trailing out of a hole in the center of the roof. It was the largest building she had ever seen. Raising the hide. Margaret saw six old men and two old women seated inside on folded blankets

As she was prodded toward this austere group, Margaret wondered at the presence of women at what was clearly a solemn occasion. Since Topknot was standing beside her, she asked him—knowing now that he spoke and probably understood a fair amount of English—what the presence of the old women was meant to signify.

In the dim light filtering through cracks in the walls, she saw that as usual he did not look at her directly or acknowledge her question. She had noticed that the Shawnee seldom looked directly at the faces of those with whom they were conversing but rather off to the side, as if out of deference. Although deference to a captive, Margaret knew, was unlikely, she determined to take it as such.

Agatha was clutching her arm. "They will kill us now, surely."

"Hardly in the council chamber," Margaret told her, her voice less assured than she wished.

"Wellett, Neeham," the oldest of the men pronounced slowly, looking for once directly at Topknot. Margaret committed the words to memory. "Inu-manila-fewam," he went on, and then, in garbled English, "Grandmother, Great Spirit, weaves skemotah." From his gestures, Margaret understood he meant that this ancient one weaves a net, and was reminded of the story of three sisters, Fates, who cut the web of life. Later, much later, after she had learned the Shawnee tongue, Margaret would understand that when Inu-manila-fewam finishes weaving the net, it is lowered to Earth, and all deemed worthy are gathered into it and translated to a place of peace and happiness.

"An old woman is their god?" Agatha asked, dismayed. "Then surely we are done for."

Overhearing her, Topknot said (and at that moment Margaret chided herself for using the ridiculous nickname), "Some old women wiser than some men."

"I never heard the like," Agatha muttered. "Our women are set to no such task."

Topknot pushed them almost to the feet of the council members.

Peering through the gloom to avoid looking at the withered faces before her, Margaret saw a white man of middle age and size, his skin so darkened by the sun, or perhaps by an application of walnut juice—she had heard of such things—that she would have taken him for an Indian, especially as he was wearing a breechcloth and moccasins. But he was staring at her intently, which no Indian would do. Over his breechcloth and partly covering it, he wore a calico shirt such as she had made more than once for her husband.

A spasm of grief seized her, but it passed quickly as the white Indian began to speak.

"They wish to question you," he said in a voice that reminded Margaret of the Irish settlers at home. "I will serve as interpreter, by your leave."

"We are grateful for your assistance," Margaret said. "I wish to show my respect by calling these people by their correct names. Who is that?" She gestured toward Topknot, having learned through observation not to point.

"Chief White Bark," the white Indian said. "You and your sister are under his protection." At that White Bark stepped back, giving place to the white Indian and an ancient elder, man or woman, Margaret could not tell, who stared directly at her and asked her a question.

"She is asking if your late husband was a captain," the white Indian told her.

Agatha was imploring her not to answer but Margaret saw no reason for that.

"No, an ordinary soldier in the militia," Margaret told the old one, who turned to the others with a dismissive gesture.

"Do not lie," the white Indian warned her.

"I am not in the habit of lying," Margaret said heatedly. "Why do they not believe me?"

"His bravery during the attack tells them he was a captain."

"Say that he was," Agatha pleaded. "It might bring us better treatment."

Margaret shook off her trembling hand.

The sisters waited while the elders continued their consultation, which the white Indian explained had to do with their adoption. So it was decided, he told her: she was to become the sister of a warrior, Wa-Ba-Kah-Kah-Ho, White Bark's son, whose sister had died recently. Another fate was planned for Agatha, who began to wail when the white Indian told her that she was to be sold. Now Margaret understood why they had been spared the gauntlet: they were precious plunder.

She took Agatha in her arms, comforting her as best she could. "Remember how often we have heard of captives sold, only to be reunited before long with their families. Your fate is far kinder than mine."

Unconvinced, Agatha went on sobbing as the two old women led Margaret out of the council house. In spite of her protests, her sister was left behind and it seemed likely that Margaret would never see her again.

Margaret was sobbing as the two women led her by her hands, without gentleness, to a clearing at some distance from the council house. Knowing how the Indians scorned any sign of weakness, Margaret was able to suppress her tears, although sobs continued to heave her.

The first old woman stripped her, marveling at the buttons on her dress and the intricacies of her undergarments. She then led Margaret down the bank to the river and dragged her in until both were submerged to the shoulders in icy water. Fetched out shivering, Margaret was dried roughly with handfuls of dead leaves. The Indian woman then wrung out Margaret's soaked garments and spread them to dry on a rock.

A second woman plucked the big leathery leaves of a dock weed growing on the bank and began to scrub Margaret with their veined undersides. She scrubbed every inch of her body, not neglecting the tender places under her arms and between her legs, and vigorously rubbing her breasts. The sensation was strong but not unpleasant. Then she scoured Margaret with a strip of bark, which caused her to shrink until she bethought herself of the natives' regard for courage and clenched her jaw and stood still. When it was done, her body was pink and striped with scratches.

Then they dressed her in a soft doeskin kilt and an overblouse of the same material, which seemed to have been made for a larger woman. They unshod her of the leather boots John had made for her before the journey; the boots were torn and stained now, but Margaret gasped with pain when the women took them away. Finally, they stepped her feet into moccasins and wrapped deerskin leggings, embroidered with blue beads, around her scratched legs. The elder Indian loosed her hair from its pins, spread it out, and marveled at its fairness, then braided it roughly in two tails that fell nearly to Margaret's waist.

Margaret had protested the loss of her undergarments but to no avail; the old women gathered them up along with her gown and breeches, indicating with gestures that they would be burned.

A wampum belt of blue and white beads was fastened around her waist and then one of the old woman produced a pot of white paint and drew a line with her forefinger from Margaret's forehead to the tip of her nose.

She felt the stripe applied and slowly drying on her skin and reached up to touch it with her fingertips. It was a slight difference, like the too-large garments—yet what a difference was there! Heretofore, hemmed in by buttons, ties, coarse seams, and high collars, she had always felt herself pinioned. Now she had a freedom that would bring, she knew, untoward consequences. She wondered what John would have said if he had seen her now, or how the infant that had nuzzled her breasts would have found its way through the deerskin.

Then the two women led Margaret back to the council house. There, she saw for the first time, the face of her new brother, Wa-Ba-Kah-Kah-Ho, White Bark's son. It was of a relentless fierceness that terrified her. His jaws were clenched, his lips slightly apart over his teeth. His cheeks were deeply scarred from smallpox.

He did not look at Margaret or speak to her but beckoned to her to follow him.

Wa-Ba-Kah-Kah-Ho led her toward the entrance of the council house. He raised the hide over the door opening, then let it fall in her face. A woman following close behind nudged Margaret forward and she lifted the hide and went in.

A crowd of Shawnee was assembling in the clearing. She saw White Bark, Brother One, and Raven Wing, as well as Uncle merged into the crowd. They did not look at her or seem to recognize her.

Five men advanced to the front of the crowd, beating a drum as big as a hogshead. They chanted monotonously as the Shawnee began to circle and dance. Their steps were like nothing Margaret had ever seen, a slow pacing that gave way suddenly to leaps and bounds. The chanting and drumming continued, monotonous, meaningless, without recognizable rhythm or tune.

After many minutes, Margaret turned away, exhausted and confused, but the two women who had bathed and dressed her snatched her by the elbows before she could make her escape and held her firmly. She was not to be granted a reprieve, and as the night deepened, she continued to stand as firmly as she could, realizing little by little that this ceremony had something to do with her adoption. She had hoped the matter was already concluded.

Later she would think her exhaustion had blinded her to the spectacle. Through the haze of her fatigue she saw only arms swinging, legs leaping, as though detached from the bodies of those who had been her enemies. She did not see their faces, did not notice the stripes and smears of red and black. Later, a huge bonfire turned them all into cavorting shadows. As the moon rose, veiled by trees, Margaret realized that the dancing was going to continue all night, with brief intervals when the braves joined the onlookers in snatching bits of meat from the boiling kettle that hung over the fire. No one offered her water or anything else to sustain her. She had only her will, strengthened by her determination to show them her courage. It was, she knew, her only hope of mercy.

Late in the night, the drummers and chanters retreated to their long houses and the audience scattered. The two old women pushed Margaret along to their place. Once inside, Margaret tried to loosen her kilt and leggings in order to lie down and sleep, but one of the old women interrupted her movements, gesturing that she must never remove what they had put on her. The garments, so old and soft, were serving a purpose she would not understand until much later when she was able to ask questions and understand the answers.

Dropping to a pad of blankets, she slept.

CHAPTER ELEVEN

MARGARET WOKE AT first light, not knowing where she was. After a moment, her eyes grew accustomed to the dimness and she recognized the long house that, she knew, would from now on be her dwelling place. Piles of blankets, a cooking pot, and various utensils were piled near the shallow pit that was now a smoldering bed of ashes.

Looking at the sleeping bodies around her, wrapped in blankets or bedrolls, Margaret estimated that twelve full-grown men and woman and an equal number of children shared this space. The long house was perhaps twenty feet long and twelve feet wide; poles divided it into spaces for each family. She was grateful for the few feet that had apparently been designated hers.

Her new brother was seated on a folded blanket at the center of the dwelling. He seemed to be lost in thought or dream, wearing only his breechcloth and beaded moccasins. Two eagle feathers rose from a knot of hair on the back of his head. The rest of his head had been shaven. The slight familiarity she had gained on the trail evaporated in the dim light. Margaret thought him a terrifying hulk, impenetrable in his strangeness.

Two Indian squaws were waking. One of them said something Margaret could not understand but which she thought might be a sort of greeting, or even a welcome. She had heard tales at home of the cruelty of the squaws to their white women captives, but in that case, nearly all of the captives had been young and, she guessed, adopted as concubines by the braves rather than as daughters. She knew she would not fall into that trap and endure the ignominy as well as the jealous rage of the squaws.

Now her new brother was looking at her as though for the first time. He said a word in Shawnee with profound emphasis, repeating it several times, that seemed to mean she was being renamed. Then he dismissed her with a wave of his hand. The two squaws led her out of the long house.

Margaret attempted to repeat the new name and to inquire about its meaning, but the squaws either did not understand her or chose to ignore her question.

In the clearing, thirty or more Shawnee were gathered, wearing what Margaret thought might be clothes for a ceremony. For a moment she imagined the ceremony might be in honor of her adoption. As the Shawnee circled, stomped, and shouted, two drummers took up the beat. Margaret and the squaws stood watching as other Shawnee gathered behind them, all watching attentively.

Then she saw Agatha led into the circle. Agatha, too, had been stripped, scrubbed, and re-clothed in deerskin kilt and moccasins. The experience seemed to have unnerved her; she looked across the circle at Margaret beseechingly, but Margaret was beginning to realize that a stern protocol governed all her movements and she did not go to her.

When the braves' dance was finished and the circle cleared, Margaret's and Agatha's squaws led their two charges to the middle of the space. As the whole tribe watched, the squaws spoke words that might belong, Margaret first thought, to a prayer or a chant—a long, low droning that might instead be a recitation of the wars, the deaths, and the captures leading to this moment: a somber account.

White Bark stepped forward and firmly placed Margaret's right hand into the hand of the squaw who stood beside her.

Then, with the same firmness, he separated Agatha's hands from the hands of her two squaws, who stepped back into the crowd.

The white Indian, Girty, stepped forward, seized Agatha's arm, and began to drag her away. Margaret lunged, but her two squaws held her back. She had never abandoned her sister during all the trials of the trail, but now she had no choice. To comfort herself, she remembered that likely captives were sometimes sold to the governor in Detroit and went into his service. She swiped the tears off her cheek. Agatha, sobbing and struggling, was dragged away.

A few minutes after she disappeared, the two squaws let go of Margaret's hands. But the whole tribe was watching her attentively. There would be no escape.

She was set to her first task immediately, sent with a group of girls to gather the last blackberries from a dense, thorny patch on the far side of the long houses. The girls chattered and laughed, quickly stripping the berries from their branches, seeming not to notice the way their arms and hands were scratched. Margaret was slower. The work gave her a chance to look all the way down what seemed to be the main street of the village, with bark-covered long houses on both sides. She was astonished to see so many—fifty at least, each a hive of activity with squaws outside, grinding corn in mortars, slicing meat, or tending to the cooking fires. The braves were nowhere to be seen.

The basket of berries she brought back to her squaw was only half full, and the woman snarled a word Margaret didn't need to translate. She would have to do better at her next task. Fatigue was no excuse nor, she guessed, was her aching back, brought on by days of riding and her delicate condition. She had suspected it since September when her courses had not returned but had laid that down to the fact that she had been nursing. Now, she knew the truth.

She did not know when it had happened, when a sharp urge had wakened John from the sodden sleep of exhaustion, but she could not remember the conception of her lost daughter either and suspected this was generally true of women who never spoke of such things. Possibly this new life was created to replace the daughter she had lost.

She wondered if she would be shown more mercy when her belly rounded but doubted it. She had noticed three squaws with big bellies working around the village, one hauling an enormous pack of firewood on her back, the other two sweeping the main street till it was free of every pebble. This was familiar from the Greenbrier Settlement, where women worked until they went into labor, and even then managed to finish whatever task they had undertaken. It was the same here.

In the afternoon two hunters brought in a large stag, slung from a sturdy branch. Several Indians came forward and the skinning, butchering, and carving began. Margaret guessed that the deer signaled a feast of some importance.

Meanwhile a group of squaws fed twigs to the fire in the center of the village and, when it was well aroused, some larger branches. They erected a spit over it and began to roast sections of meat.

The smell of roasting meat made Margaret's mouth water; she could not remember how long it had been since she had eaten. Trying to calm her hunger, she opened her mouth and swallowed a large mouthful of air, cool and almost liquid. It did no good, serving only to remind her that winter was coming with fierce cold she would have to find ways to survive. All hope of a swift rescue had floated away when they crossed the big river, and she knew she would never survive an escape alone through the wilderness.

When the meat was ready, one of her squaws brought her a choice bit of haunch. As Margaret began to tear it with her teeth, the squaw removed the meat from her hands. When she handed it back, Margaret understood that she was meant to eat more slowly, for health or for ritual, or possibly for both.

Her appetite was rapidly satisfied. She looked at the woman who had taken the meat away, seeing in her wizened face a look so neutral, so lacking in obvious meaning that she felt a distance like a cold draft between them. Nevertheless, she asked her, "Where is my sister?" but the woman, who either knew no English or did not chose to respond, looked away.

Margaret snatched another bit of deer meat from the cooking pot of the squaw she had named Mary Rabbit because of her long ears. She scorched her fingers, but she was so hungry she did not notice the pain. Then she was sent off to scrub a filthy blanket in the icy water at the edge of the river—the Ohio, she said to herself, with satisfaction. Knowing the name of the river comforted her, at least for the moment.

After sunset and a mouthful of corn porridge, Margaret went to settle herself for the night. Her squaw watched her neatly spread her blanket and settle herself in a fold. Then the old woman turned away and began to gather her children and bed them down in the next section. There were four children, close in age, the youngest hardly more than an infant, which surprised Margaret since her squaw seemed to be too old. But perhaps Indian women who looked so wrinkled were actually worn by work and not by age. From her blanket, Margaret watched her squaw lace her sleeping infant onto a cradle board, which she hung from a nail on the post. The next smallest child she huddled inside her blanket, while the other two were left to sprawl where they could. Stricken with exhaustion, Margaret hardly heard the footsteps of other Shawnee coming in and settling to sleep.

In the dark of the night, a little child crawled to Margaret and she extended her left arm to hold it.

Half awake, Margaret realized that the closeness of silent breathing bodies, even though the bodies were those of savages, was curiously consoling. She remembered the loft in the cabin at home where she had been packed in to sleep along with the other children. Their bodies and their breathing had comforted her; she had not expected to find that comfort again unless by some miracle she was restored to the Greenbrier Settlement.

Once, during the night, she was wakened by the sounds of copulation, subdued but unmistakable. She plunged back into sleep before the intercourse ended.

Dawn came with gray light and a chill breeze through the wall cracks, overcoming with scents of resin, the musky smell of the sleepers. Carefully moving her arm from under the sleeping child, Margaret crawled to her pack and withdrew her almanack, quill pen, and vial of pokeberry ink.

As the sleepers around her began to stir and rise, she opened the almanack at random and read, "Fear not death, for the sooner we die, the longer we will be immortal." Mr. Franklin's words, she thought, should be addressed to Agatha, not to her. She did not expect to see her sister again, nor did she have any notion of what dangers Agatha would face if she was taken to Detroit to be sold. She still hoped that her sister's fair face might persuade one of the white men there to marry her.

Thinking of her sister sold like a slave, Margaret's tears dropped onto the page, moistening the small space where she had intended to write. Wiping her eyes with the back of her hand, she turned the page and read, "Hear no ill of a friend, or speak any of an enemy."

Underneath it she wrote in neat small script, "In the village at last. All is unknown."

She became aware of being watched. Wa-Ba-Kah-Kah-Ho had risen from his bedroll to see what she was doing. He said in clear, although strangely accented English, "You write. You teach."

A sense of calm slowed Margaret's breathing. She knew there was safety in the task. The Shawnee needed to know how to read and write, if only to sign their names on the documents white men gave them. Perhaps they would even grow proficient enough to read what they were signing.

But then she foresaw a difficulty. If they could read the white men's writing, would they refuse to sign?

CHAPTER TWELVE

O N MARGARET'S SECOND DAY in the village, she found a young Shawnee man in the long house when she returned from her morning duties. He was hardly more than a boy and although his face was comely, he did not possess the adult braves' distinction, being small and scrawny. To Margaret's amazement, he held out his right hand and introduced himself: "Robert Dean. I speak English and Shawnee. I have lived with this tribe since I was eight years old."

"Captured?" Margaret asked.

"Yes, with my family, in a wagon train coming down from Fort Pitt. My father was killed, the rest of 'em died later. I like it here pretty well," he added laconically. "White Bark gave me a new name."

Here, Margaret thought, was someone who could explain the tribe's strange ways. But he was painted and dressed like a young brave, and although his skin was white, she wondered where his loyalty lay.

"What is your Shawnee name?" she asked.

"I will tell you when you are able to say it."

"Did they take you into a family?"

"Jimmo White. I am now his son who was killed at the battle of Fort Stanwix, when we tried to make a confederacy, claim the Ohio as our boundary, but they broke us at Fallen Timbers."

"I heard of that. Were you in that fight?"

He shook his head. "Too young. Jimmo keeps me close, afraid to lose another son. But I am strong!" he insisted. "I'll fight the next one, drive them Long Knives back to Virginia!"

"Those are my people," Margaret said stiffly.

Robert smiled. "Not no more, Missy. These here are your people."

"Never," Margaret said. "I'll get back to the Greenbrier Settlement some way."

"They don't like to sell us back, once we are part of a family. I never have known it to happen, even when the ransom money is big."

"I don't understand," Margaret said angrily. Robert Dean's certainty annoyed her. "They must know we don't belong here."

He leaned against the door post, settling in for a long gab. "Look at it this way," he said. "The Shawnee have lost a whole lot—not only their warriors but their women and children. Fighting, sickness, starvation. They need us to replace the dead ones. That's why they dress us in their clothes and give us new names."

Margaret cringed. Now she understood why the garments she'd been given were too big and why they were worn soft with use.

"I will teach you Indian words," Robert Dean volunteered. "But not yet. You would not know how to say them. And you will teach them how to write. I know already," he added proudly.

"How is it that you are schooled?"

"Blue Jacket's wife, a white woman, schoolteacher long ago on the other side of the mountains. I will take you to meet her." He was turning away.

"Where is my sister?" Margaret asked hastily. "Will she be adopted too?"

Robert shrugged. "I hear they've taken her to Detroit, maybe to the governor. She has a pretty face," he added matter-of-factly.

"Is there nothing more to it?" Margaret cried, but Robert Dean was already walking away.

<hr>

As the early days of winter passed, Margaret noticed that she was being allowed a degree of freedom. She was usually watched by one or another of the squaws, but they were at the same time busy with their work, preparing what provisions they had on hand for the season of hardship to come. There were piles of corn to shuck, shell, and grind with mortars and pestles, then pack in homespun bags and hang from the poles at the top of the long houses. Margaret was given the task of packing the bags because of her small hands, with fierce reprimands if she spilled as much as a grain.

Stepping outside to relieve herself, Margaret saw that labor of various sorts but all with the same aim was going on throughout the camp. Sides of meat, buffalo, deer, and antelope, were being smoked over fires banked down with wet wood for the purpose, the meat then hung high at the tops of the long houses. The last of the root vegetables, the pumpkins, squash, and potatoes, were sorted then buried in an earthen pit, to freeze there and keep all winter.

Meanwhile, the braves were occupied with what appeared to Margaret to be a curious sort of game. Armed with long sticks, a group of ten or twelve gathered in the center of the village every evening. An old man tossed a ball up and the combatants tried to catch it with their sticks and knock it away. Margaret was digging potatoes in a patch overlooking the village and she could see the men, sweating, straining, beating the ball away with their sticks with what appeared to be a sort of good-humored combativeness.

Little Mouse, seeing her watching, hustled her away, her little eyes shining like a mouse recovering crumbs as they had that first night together in the long house when Margaret had given her her name.

The next day, Margaret saw with astonishment a group of men and women playing a game together, hiding some sort of metal disk in their hands and trying to mislead their opponents, who darted in and out, attempting to find the object. This was the first time Margaret had heard her captors laugh aloud. Having grown up hearing tales of their cruel solemnity, she could hardly believe her ears. What's more, men and women playing a game together was something she had never seen before.

As evening came on, drummers took up their places and the slow, somber beat began. Chanting followed as men and women came out of the long houses and formed two circles, the men in the inner circle, the women outside. Round and round they went, first in one direction, then in the reverse. Little Mouse joined the outer circle, pacing in one direction, then the other, and for the first time, Margaret was not being watched. A thought flashed across her mind: she could make her escape, running unobserved to the edge of the village and then disappearing into the trees.

She stood frozen. It was a moment that seemed, briefly, to be of major importance. And yet she could not move. The thought of forcing her way alone through the wilderness, without provisions or water, terrified her, but there was something else holding her back.

She ran her hands along her soft deerskin kilt, even reaching down to touch the blue beads on her leggings. She did not know the name of the dead woman whose clothes she was wearing, but they were holding her in place. She could not flee.

Was it loyalty to these wild beings, she wondered? That would indeed be strange. She knew them as murderers, plunderers, destroyers of villages and of lives. Yet there was something that held her here, even against her will. It was like the monotonous beating of the drums that sometimes seemed to follow the beating of her heart. She belonged here, in this barbarous place, as she had never belonged in the Greenbrier.

She sensed that her connection had been forged during the first week of her captivity by Little Mouse and the other silent, watchful women—the kweewe, as she had heard them called. Now, with their attention for once distracted, she felt a curious fluttering, as though her heartstrings were being plucked. Yet she could not flee. She stood still and silent, watching the dance.

Finally, when it was almost over, a young kweewe joined the onlookers, carrying an infant in her arms. Margaret saw that the infant was wearing her murdered daughter's smock.

Tearing at her hair she began to scream.

Immediately, she was surrounded. She pointed at the baby, gasping and screaming. Tears shot out of her eyes and streamed down her cheeks.

The woman carrying the baby was hustled away. Margaret never saw that little white smock again.

Now her grieving began in force. She had hardly mourned the sickly infant snatched from her arms, comforting herself with the knowledge that this one would not have survived the winter. She had grieved for the baby's past, so short, so uncertain, but not for her unimagined future.

Now she saw her daughter as she might have become in time: at two years old, crawling around the cabin; at four, scurrying to meet her father when John came in from hunting; and even further along, a blossoming maiden with their small world expanding to meet her. Now she grieved all the growth that could not be, the future murdered along with her daughter.

She stumbled back to the long house and lay down on her blanket, utterly desolate. Her tears dried without soothing her pain. She knew it would be with her for the rest of her life, waning when she was working or otherwise distracted, returning full force as she fell asleep at night or woke in the morning—always the image of her lost daughter growing and grown.

When she had lain there for an hour, Little Mouse came with a bitter tea, which she spooned into Margaret's mouth. Although she did not want it, the effect was immediate. She scrambled to her feet.

With gestures, Little Mouse indicated that Margaret must now go outside. Knowing there was kindness in this invitation, Margaret went out and found Robert Dean waiting for her. Without explanation he led her and Little Mouse into the forest.

When they came to a clearing, she saw looming in front of them a large wooden house. A row of columns supported the roof of a commodious porch, and the windows on the ground floor had both wooden shutters and leaded glass. She knew at once that the house must be the abode of a great chief, or of a white man.

This last idea she soon dismissed as Robert led her and Little Mouse into a front hall with a tall ceiling, whitewashed walls, and a large window giving a view of the surrounding forest. Boldly placed by the fire, a red-jacketed brave rocked and regarded them.

She studied the man in the rocking chair with disbelief. He wore a red military jacket with gold epaulets and wide velvet lapels and cuffs. Large silver bracelets circled his wrists, and around his neck he wore a silver ornament on a beaded string. His hair was cut short and his handsome face was not marred by smallpox.

"Why stare at me, white woman?" he asked in English muddied by a strange accent.

Margaret summoned her courage. "I have never seen one of your kind dressed in such a way. Are you a chief?"

"You white people call me Chief Blue Jacket, but my jacket is red."

"Like the British," Margaret said, greatly hazarding. "The invaders."

"Most useful allies," the man said, rocking away, "at least at certain times."

"The British do not burn our towns," Margaret hazarded.

He gestured impatiently. "You burn my towns. You kill my people. My town, where you are living now, was burned twice. Our women and children were shot down when they tried to run to the woods."

Margaret raised her hand to protest—she had never heard of such a deed—but she was interrupted when a young white woman came into the room with a tray of tea things. Margaret noticed with astonishment the porcelain cups decorated with pink moss roses. (Most, however, were chipped or had lost their saucers.) A matching teapot stood over the cups, although it had no top. The white woman set the tray on a table and began rapidly filling the cups.

When she passed one to Margaret, she saw the woman's blue eyes.

"Who are you?" Margaret asked.

"Sarah Moore, captured in the year of famine, twelve moons ago. I am married to Blue Jacket," she added with a degree of pride, and Margaret noticed that her belly was round under her deer-skin jerkin and remembered Robert Dean saying, "They need us to replace their dead."

Margaret judged that Sarah Moore was perhaps twenty years younger than Blue Jacket, so there would be many more babies if Sarah remained with the tribe as seemed likely. Also, she realized that Sarah might become a valuable friend, even an ally, a source of assistance in time of trouble. She touched the woman's arm as she turned away. "What is this tea?" she asked. It was nearly as dark as whiskey.

"Good India tea, bought with six scalps from the British trader in Detroit," Sarah said.

Margaret pushed on. "What is that silver disk your husband wears around his neck?"

"The face of our English father, our King George," Sarah replied, moving away to serve the others.

"He is not *our* father," Margaret told her. "We settlers want no king."

Sarah did not reply.

Now it was clear: Blue Jacket and his people were allies of the invading British, thus his big house and evident prosperity. Margaret had heard that the British were generous to their native allies who had helped them in many wars. Looking around the room, she saw a portrait of a white man in a ruffled shirt over the mantel of the big stone fireplace, surely some British nobleman. The screen before the fire was finely wrought, as were the walnut chairs with their high backs and pillowed seats. Margaret had never expected to see an Indian living higher on the hog than any white man.

But Blue Jacket must have prospered by betraying his people, for she had heard that the British abandoned their Indian allies as soon as they proved no longer useful, and often turned on them with ferocity. What use, then, of the porcelain tea service and the portrait of the white man over the mantel?

She was not shocked or even surprised. Everyone must prove useful in this place, and she felt a sharp thrust of anxiety. What was her use and for how much longer would she be tolerated, eating their meat and sleeping by their fires? Even when she worked all day, packing bags with cornmeal, she hardly matched the industry of the kweewe.

To soothe herself, she sipped her smoky tea, her first real India tea, as two children came into the room, boys of five and six, and ran to Blue Jacket. They were brought in by Robert Dean. He greeted Sarah and Blue Jacket with a degree of familiarity Margaret had not seen before and was answered in the same vein, Blue Jacket even releasing his boys to extend his hand.

Now Sarah passed around a tray of little cakes made with fine white flour, and Margaret, always hungry, took three. Robert, who was watching her, frowned. "You eat too much," he said. "It is not the way here." And, indeed, Blue Jacket and his sons took only one cake each, eating it slowly while Margaret devoured her handful.

"You must be mindful of your position," Robert scolded her with the assurance of a very young man. "You are never safe here."

"But I am always hungry," Margaret protested, "and there are plenty of these cakes."

"Strive to be of more use," Robert told her. His solemn tone frightened Margaret and she got up to gather the teacups and carry them to the kitchen, but a black woman in an apron and cap took the tray out of her hands and Margaret realized with renewed astonishment that Blue Jacket owned a slave.

Still frightened—for Robert's voice seemed to be the voice of her own fear—Margaret looked at the whitewashed wall and saw a slate hanging from a nail with a bit of chalk. Her mother's voice returned: "Teach, Margaret, Teach."

She turned to Robert. "That slate—" Before she could ask, he handed it down to her with its chalk. Curious, the two little boys left their father and came to her.

"I will teach your sons to write, with your permission," she told Blue Jacket.

He said, "It is needed. Your Long Knives give us many papers and we sign with our marks, not knowing what words they contain."

They are not my Long Knives, Margaret thought, knowing it was heresy.

She propped the slate on her knee and drew a large *A*. "A," she told the two boys. "Now you copy it."

The older of the two, his fair hair already long on his shoulders, leaned over the slate and reached for the chalk. He drew an *A* with one lame leg.

As she rubbed out the lame leg and replaced it with a straight one, Margaret remembered her own primer. "A is for apple," she said.

The younger boy, slight as an elf, took the chalk from his brother and drew a ladder, the sides not meeting at the top. Again Margaret rubbed out the attempt, replacing it with a proper *A*.

"And *A* is for *armadillo*," she instructed, then realized the word would not be familiar to them. "A is for *anvil*," she substituted, having seen one in the camp.

The boys stared at her.

"What are their names?" she asked Blue Jacket, but his answers were incomprehensible.

"She does not yet speak Shawnee," Robert explained to the chief unnecessarily. Margaret was beginning to find the young white man a nuisance. "You may call the elder Peter," Robert told her, "and John the younger." Margaret knew the boys would not answer to either name and realized that she could take no more time in learning their language.

The older boy was covering the slate with white scrawls, and Margaret was concerned for her chalk, which was rapidly diminishing. She pried it from his fingers, then wiped the slate clean with the side of her hand.

"*B*," she said as she wrote it, then passed the slate. "*B* is for . . ." She remembered that in her primer, *B* had stood for *butter*, but that would have no meaning for these boys. "*B* is for *bear*," she said.

Now Little Mouse came forward and indicated with a wave of her arm that it was time to go. Margaret left the two boys reluctantly. The warm pressure as they leaned against her knees had reminded her of her little brothers, crowding about her in the evenings at home, coaxing a story. She had forgotten how much she had enjoyed that warmth, the musty smell of their fair hair and the clutch of their hands.

Rising from her chair, Margaret turned to Blue Jacket. "I will come every day to teach them, with your permission." He nodded. She looked the same question to Sarah, who smiled with something that reminded Margaret of gratitude.

"I taught my husband and a few others when I first came here," Sarah said, "but now there is too much to do, preparing for winter. I have a primer saved from my days as a schoolteacher in Virginia. I will give it to you."

Blue Jacket said, "Tanakia westre catuelo k weshe lavishph."

Robert translated, "We are strong when we do what is right."

Afterward, Robert Dean seemed impressed by the exchange he had witnessed. Outside the house, he told Margaret, "A very great chief, Blue Jacket. A few years back, he refused to bow to the white captain they call Mad Anthony when he came demanding the Ohio Country. We had war and loss because of that, but still, a very great chief."

<hr/>

Before she could return to Blue Jacket's house, the first storm of winter covered the village with a foot of snow and obscured the dim path through the woods to the clearing.

Finding herself confined to the long house, Margaret turned to another task, cutting the lengths of calico Little Mouse had traded for with a white man passing through from Detroit. Margaret had noted Little Mouse's skill in trading, even though she shared no language with the white man; she conveyed her wishes clearly enough with gestures and expressions. The trader, a squat white man with large dirty hands that smudged the calico, tried to best Little Mouse without success. At last accepting as payment, although with bad grace, two big sacks of late corn and squash, the white man had stomped out of the long house, leaving behind several lengths of calico and a sour stink that reminded Margaret of home.

White Bark came to be measured for a shirt, greeting Margaret with a word she recognized as her new name. His kindness was measured, but it reassured her: after all, she had been adopted into his family and wore his murdered daughter's clothes. Perhaps the kinship would protect her to some degree.

Measuring without a tape, Margaret used her hands, moving them rapidly over White Bark's shoulders, chest, and arms as he flinched and scowled. A word from Little Mouse caused him to stand still for her touch. At the finish, Margaret had only a rough estimate of his size, but it would have to do. As soon as he had left, she laid out a length of calico on the floor, measured it with her hands, and began to cut with the scissors that she had kept safe in her housewife, along with needles and thread.

As she was cutting, somewhat fearfully—for she might spoil the material—she heard a commotion outside the cabin. Then three young kweewe carried in the husk of an old woman.

Margaret, starting up, thought at first that the woman was dead, but her eyelids were trembling and a bit of breath escaped her lips. She recognized her as Waban, White Bark's mother, widow of the murdered chief, Cornstalk, whom the Long Knives had betrayed.

"Lay her down here," Margaret commanded, clearing a space on the floor. She had no idea what she could do for the old woman, but since her visit to Blue Jacket's house and her first teaching, her assurance had risen up with force, and she knew the Shawnee had noticed.

When the old woman had been stretched by the fire, Margaret knelt beside her and began to chafe her clammy hands. The woman stirred and opened her eyes, then started to cough spasmodically, blood spattering her lips.

Margaret recognized the signs, dreaded above all in old people. Her grandmother had died of it. Pneumonia.

She still wore around her neck the deerskin bag her mother had given her on parting, filled with dried herbs potent enough to ward off and even at times to cure sickness. It still contained a half cup of the herbs.

Unknotting the cord, she took the bag down and opened it. The tawny smell of the dried herbs filled the room. "Hot water," she commanded in Shawnee, her second and third words.

One of the attendant women filled an iron kettle from the crock and hung it on the tripod over the fire. Margaret took the kettle down and set it in the coals. In a matter of minutes, steam rose from the spout. She snatched up a gourd dipper lying by the fire, poured a spoonful of her herbs into it, and added the boiling water. Steam rose up from the gourd and a sweet nut-like smell filled the room.

When the tea had cooled a little, she began to spoon it into the old woman's mouth, prying her jaws apart. Waban sputtered, coughed, and sat up to ward off the gourd, but one of the women held her upright while another captured her flailing hands. Margaret poured rapidly, some of the tea spilling on the frail old neck, where the coughing seemed lodged. When the gourd was empty, the two women laid Waban back down by the fire. She grimaced, clutched her hands, and fell into a deep sleep. "She will recover now," Margaret said, having no idea whether that would be the outcome.

That night the sick woman stayed in Margaret's long house, and as the others came in to sleep, Margaret hushed them, pointing to her patient. She managed to wake herself every few hours to brew more tea, waving the steam with a feather toward the old woman's clogged nostrils. Now she swallowed the tea with less resistance.

At dawn Robert Dean came in on one of his inspection tours. He crouched, studying Waban. "You have made her better," he concluded. He seemed impressed.

In the morning, Waban scrambled to her feet. She was not coughing. She reached for Margaret's hands and pressed them firmly. Then she was on her way.

Margaret knew she was far from healed, but at least the first step was taken. She knelt on the floor by the abandoned calico and began to cut it.

CHAPTER THIRTEEN

MARGARET RECOGNIZED HER good fortune when, by the time of the first full moon of the new year, Waban was fully recovered. The story of her healing spread rapidly through the village, and Margaret knew there would be other calls for her herbal remedy. Earlier, she had recognized two of the herbs, houndstooth and purslane, growing at the edge of the village, but now they were covered with snow and she would not be able to pluck and dry their leaves to add to her little pouch. Meanwhile, she had used the last of the precious herbs her mother had given her to help Waban and her pouch was now empty.

Fearing what might happen as word of the healing spread, she asked Little Mouse, who often spoke in council, to explain that the white sister could only heal infants or very old people, leaving the others to be saved by traditional means, such as the sweat lodge and the rituals of the medicine man and woman. Little Mouse told her that there was some grumbling at this news, but since Margaret's authority in the matter of healing was not questioned, her rule held.

Next she gathered strips of yellow birch and alder bark, shredding them and boiling them with a drop of her hoarded honey to make a tea. She was able to bring two babies through sieges of croup and to lessen the suffering of three elders on their death beds.

White Bark, watching her boil the tea, reached out his right hand, touched her shoulder, and said the strange words of her new name, which Robert Dean translated for her. "Why does he call me Little Ship Under Full Sail?" she asked Robert; he was sharpening his hunting knife on the other side of the fire. "These are people of creeks, streams, and rivers, with no occasion to see a sailing ship."

"One of their myths tells that long ago they lived by a great water, perhaps one of the northern lakes, in truth an inland sea," he explained.

"Why is this name given to me?"

"You are noted for moving rapidly, like a ship under full sail."

Now that she understood the meaning, Margaret was glad to accept her new name. In the evening as she fell asleep, she repeated it. The words took the place of the prayers she was beginning to forget.

<hr/>

The deepening cold and heavy snows of late winter were hard on the Shawnee. Hunters ploughed through the shrouded woods in search of game but came back with only a few scrawny rabbits and squirrels, blaming, as always, the Long Knives, although none had been seen in this Ohio country for a long time. The women made do with that meat and whatever they had saved in the autumn— roots, and corn kernels they ground into flour. Mixed with water, a little salt—which was carefully rationed, since a visit to the Blue Licks would be required to fetch more—the cakes were cooked on griddles over the fires and eaten with boiled carrots, potatoes, and squash. Margaret noticed that everyone was growing thin. She was hungry to the point of desperation, waking up during the frigid nights to nurse her swollen belly with both arms.

Little Mouse noticed her condition. She began sharing her meager portion of food. Margaret tried to refuse, but her need was too great as well as the need of the infant she was carrying, who might die in her womb for lack of nourishment. Although she tried to wish for its death in this unforgiving place, she was not able to maintain that resolve, even knowing that the kweewe had several potent herbs to bring on miscarriage.

The biting cold gave the tribe not the infections of the warm months but something quieter and more deadly: starvation, and the fevers attendant on it. White Bark's brother His Bad Horse succumbed to the coughing sickness, three kweewe went down to starvation, and Margaret was able to save only the two infants; four others perished. Yet even that saving was considered a miracle, and she was now treated with great and unexpected respect.

On a day of early thaw when the roofs of the long houses were dripping melt water that drilled round holes into the fallen snow, a woman came to the cabin carrying an infant laced onto a cradleboard.

Margaret, who had been stripping locust bark to add to the pot of water boiling on the fire, sprang to her feet. The woman held out the cradleboard and Margaret saw that the baby was about the age of her murdered daughter. She was asleep, her small face flushed with fever. Her limbs were firmly encased in the bindings of the cradleboard, and Margaret gestured to the mother to unloose them. She was unwilling and took a step backward.

"What is this woman's name?" Margaret asked Little Mouse, who was standing close by.

"Wa-Ka-Be-Nu-Pa," Little Mouse said, beginning to unwrap the infant. "She is afraid."

"I see that," Margaret said more sharply than she had intended. As Little Mouse unwound the child, she awoke and began to wail feebly, raising her small hands. The mother loosened her tunic and offered her breast, but the infant turned her head away, too weak to pull on the nipple.

With Little Mouse translating, Margaret asked when this illness had begun and was shocked to hear that the baby had been failing for two months, since the first big snow of December. The mother had been too afraid of the white woman to turn to her for help, and it was only when the rituals of the medicine woman failed that she mastered her fear.

Margaret picked up the little girl and rocked her in her arms. The feeble wails died and the pitiful being lapsed into what might be the sleep of death. Feeling her slight weight in her arms, Margaret sobbed. Her own child had weighed no more on the night before she was murdered but she had imparted the same warmth to her mother's arms.

"Fetch a little of my tea," Margaret instructed Little Mouse. The infant was too weak to nurse, but she was able to suck on a tiny pouch of the bark tea when Margaret pushed it into her mouth.

At once she sank back into sleep. Margaret removed the pouch from the small sagging mouth and watched the mother wrap the baby up again. Through Little Mouse, she instructed the mother to take the pouch and a gourdful of the tea and administer it every few hours.

Bowed with sorrow and fear, the mother had not dared to look at Margaret before, but now she raised her face with a flash of hope and expressed her gratitude with words Margaret was able to understand.

In the months since her capture, Margaret realized that the Shawnee language she overheard every day had seeped through her skin and into her veins, coloring her blood and loosening her tongue.

The sick baby improved a little over the winter and the mother continued to bring her to Margaret, more for what she seemed to believe was the benefit of Margaret's company than for anything further she could do. By summer the baby would be dead, but Little Mouse told Margaret the tribe believed she had gained the infant five months of life.

Anxious about becoming less useful now that her supply of herbs was used up Margaret asked her friends among the kweewe to bring her pupils who wished to learn to read. The men were not willing to spend time with a white woman but the children, confined by bad weather, were restless and eager and it became possible to assemble a class of five or six small ones nearly every day. There was no paper in the camp and the only slate Margaret knew of was kept, like a precious token, at Blue Jacket's, where she went every third day to teach his boys.

But it was possible, Margaret found, to trace the letters of the alphabet in the dirt floor of the long house with a sharpened stick. After the children learned their letters, Margaret traced a few essential words with her stick. The children began to regard her stick with awe as though it was the teacher. Fostering this notion, she stored it at night tied with a thong tied to a pole.

One dawn, she heard the familiar drone of Shawnee prayer and saw Little Mouse kneeling under the stick. So the stick was blessed with power and her pupils were even afraid of it. She had only to lift it over their heads for any commotion to cease at once.

She was exhausted at the end of each day, for teaching did not relieve her of her other chores, cooking and cleaning and going out to dig the frozen earth for roots. Anxiety about her sister visited her rarely; she had confidence that Agatha had found a way of living wherever she was. She had always been sturdy as well as stubborn, a combination that might save her life.

CHAPTER FOURTEEN

BY THE TIME the last of the spring storms had passed, two more elders had starved to death, even, Margaret heard from Little Mouse, refusing all nourishment they believed should go to the young warriors. The death of the last of these, old Wa-Ma-Pa-Suke, arrived when Margaret knew that her time was almost upon her.

She asked Little Mouse to help her during her confinement, her Shawnee now adequate to express what she would need: a kettle of hot water, the fire built up, and her blanket spread beside it.

Little Mouse said quietly, "That is not our way. I will take you to the birthing place."

"Surely not outside! The nights are still sharp, and I will need your assistance."

Little Mouse shook her head. "That is not our way."

Margaret remembered seeing White Bark's young wife, already groaning in labor, led off into the woods, not to return for ten days. And then had come the ritual cleansing in the women's sweat lodge and the dancing and chanting that seemed more to welcome her back into the tribe than to celebrate the birth of her daughter.

And so it was to be with her, she realized. She owed her life to the fact that she was an adopted member of the tribe. She could not hope to escape its ways.

A few days later, Little Mouse knew even before Margaret

did that her time had come. She folded several blankets around a load of wood, gathered a tinderbox and a good portion of jerky, and filled a bucket with water. Then she held out her hand to help Margaret up from the dirt floor. It was the first touch and the last.

Bowed low, her arms cradling her heavy belly, Margaret followed Little Mouse into the woods. She struggled slowly through a dense thicket, tripping over roots, Little Mouse marching ahead with no backward glance. Finally, at a small clearing, Little Mouse stopped, dropped her load, and began swiftly cutting limbs from the surrounding trees with her stout knife. Margaret had seen her use it before at a butchering with great dexterity but not with the speed she now displayed, the long blade flashing.

Little Mouse forced the ends of the limbs into the dirt, requiring Margaret to stand up and hold the limbs together at their tops. After she had tied the tops with a leather thong, Little Mouse ran a stout branch through them, securing its ends to two trees. Then she began to thatch the structure with vines, interweaving them with the supporting poles. Again, she commanded Margaret to help her and, subduing her moans, she complied.

The little hut was completed before the sun was high, and with her first sense of relief that day, Margaret crawled inside. Little Mouse had made a soft couch of vines and dead leaves and Margaret stretched herself on it, her cramped body beginning to release. Little Mouse set her bucket of water where Margaret could reach it with a dipping gourd—precious drops, which Margaret knew she must horde. Then, without a word or a look, Little Mouse turned back toward the village.

Margaret wanted to cry out, to plead with her to stay, but it would have done no good. In a brief moment of clarity, she remembered the old man, Joshua Owens, who had crept out of the Greenbrier Settlement one bitter night to die alone in the forest. She remembered being shocked that the old man had chosen to die without a word of kindness or affection. Now, as she was seized by a severe pain, she understood. Best to plunge into suffering and endure it alone.

Her water burst, soaking her legs and the blanket, and she knew it was time to go to work to deliver the baby as quickly as possible. Her mother when her time had come had been attended by two neighbors who had pulled her babies from her womb; her protests had done no good. Perhaps their intervention had been necessary, even life-saving, but Margaret was glad she would not have to deal with any such forceful interference.

She stood up, then squatted, reached for the stout pole at the top of the hut and began to pull down. She pulled, released, panted, and pulled again as evening came on and she heard a wolf howl in the nearby forest. She had heard that wolves were drawn by the smell of afterbirth and would even attempt to invade a cabin where a birth had taken place. By now her legs were covered with blood and she reached down for a handful of leaves to try to clean herself and blot the puddle of blood on the pallet. She gave up as her blood continued to fall.

Trying to recall the birth of her first child, she realized that the baby's death had eaten away the memory and wondered if that was the reason she had so seldom mourned.

Exhausted, she sipped from the gourd and felt the water cold and metallic against her teeth. Then a rising tide of pain swept through her and she pulled on the birthing pole, groaning and screaming, and felt the baby slide out.

Quickly, she crouched and cupped her hands to receive it. It was small because of the winter's starving time. It scarcely filled her two hands, but it was alive and already opening its tiny mouth to howl. She saw it was a boy.

Crouching, she chewed off the umbilical cord with her teeth. "I will name you John, in honor of your father," she said.

Clutching the tiny thing to her side, she collapsed on the leaves and closed her eyes. If the wolves came, they would have to take them both.

It was deep night when she was awakened by her infant's mewling. She laid it to her stiff breast and felt it draw the thin cloudy liquid that came before the milk. All that long night, waking to her infant's cries, feeding it, then falling asleep, she set the pattern of the next nights and days. From time to time, she chewed on the jerky Little Mouse had brought; it seemed sufficient to satisfy her hunger.

Spring rain was spattering on the hut when Margaret woke completely. The rain had found a crack between the vines overhead and was soaking her left shoulder. The weather was turning colder, and Margaret knew she would have to see to herself. Scrambling up, still clutching the sleeping infant, she gathered handfuls of leaves to plug the hole in the vines. Then she gathered three of the logs Little Mouse had carried in her pack and after many essays with the tinderbox managed to make a small fire in the middle of the hut.

The smoke made her cough and she was concerned for her infant. She scrabbled a small hole at the top of the hut and most of the smoke drifted out. As the hut grew warmer, she knelt by the little fire and, after laying her infant near it, held out her hands to the small flames. Later, she had to close the hole with leaves to keep out the rain.

She knew enough of Shawnee ways to guess that Little Mouse would not come to fetch her for some days. That was how the Shawnee dealt with anything they considered unclean. Women on their moons went to a lodge far off in the woods and did not return for seven suns. Women giving birth seemed to disappear and no one asked for them; they generally returned after about fourteen days. She was going to be alone in the hut for some time.

Margaret knew she would have to rouse herself to fetch more wood since she had only one small log left for the fire. Looking out the door opening, she saw that the rain had stopped and the early morning was clear, still, and cool. She wrapped the baby in a corner of her blanket and left him as she stumbled out to break small limbs and twigs from the nearby trees.

Bringing them in and stoking the fire, she began to feel hungry and felt around in Little Mouse's pack until she found the rest of the jerky. She tore at it with her teeth and felt the prickle of her first milk coming in.

All was as it should be.

CHAPTER FIFTEEN

T HE MOON HAD been a sliver the night John was born; Margaret had seen it tossed in the tops of the bare trees when she went out of the hut to relieve herself. As the moon thickened, she hoped that Little Mouse would return when the moon was full, but its fullness had passed along with three more nights of darkness before Little Mouse pushed through the door hole.

John was asleep on the pallet. Little Mouse knelt beside him, studying his face, then lifted and uncurled each of his hands. She undid the belly band Margaret had torn from her petticoat, studied the crooked knot Margaret had made at the base of his birth cord, and then replaced the strip with a clean length of cloth from her pack. Before she swaddled him, she scrutinized his body as though she was looking for a sign. Wrapping him up again, she lifted him in her arms and Margaret followed her out of the tent.

At the village, Little Mouse paraded John from lodge to lodge and the kweewe, coming out, exclaimed at what they seemed to perceive as the baby's uniqueness. Margaret had seen no other newborn welcomed in this way. The attention made her proud but also anxious. What could it portend?

She followed the kweewe who were heading to the center of the village, laughing and singing. Even Win-I-Too, the medicine woman, joined with her rattles. Margaret hoped that her baby was looked upon as a good omen. Perhaps he would prove to be a link to the Long Knives who some of the peace-making women still hoped to persuade to stop their raiding. Indeed, one of the first words Margaret had learned, eavesdropping at the edge of the council tent, had been the Shawnee for "truce."

After a few days, she realized with dismay that the village believed her baby was White Bark's grandson, fruit of one of his sons and so greeted as a future leader of the tribe. She had no words to explain that he was her husband, John's, son, and after a while she accepted that this misunderstanding might prove to be helpful to them both.

During the following weeks, Margaret acknowledged with a degree of comfort that her baby belonged to the tribe rather than to her alone. It was convenient. There was always an extra pair of hands to swaddle him or wash his cloths, a woman to carry him on his cradleboard (a habit Margaret had at the first resisted, not wishing for her son the flattened head the Shawnee prized), even milk from Nonee-Lee-Wa's breasts on a day when Margaret's nipples were too sore to nurse. Nonee-Lee-Wa was Little Mouse's daughter. Her own infant had died a week earlier and Little John relieved her swollen breasts of the unneeded milk.

Margaret finally recognized the usefulness of the cradleboard, which freed her hands for her tasks and could be hung up on a roof-supporting pole at night. When she examined the back of John's head, it did not seem to be flattening, and she guessed that the rounded skull he had inherited from his father governed the outcome.

Her resistance to these Shawnee ways faded entirely when she remembered how her mother had warned her when she found

Margaret rocking her first infant, the little daughter murdered on the trail. "Never forget," she'd said, "that many die before their second year. Do not become too attached." Like Nancy's injunction to "Teach, Margaret. Teach," this grim reminder was in tune with Margaret's new life, where so many infants died without undue mourning, their mothers becoming pregnant soon after.

By early summer, she knew she had no reason to fear that John would die—he was filling out, bright-eyed and alert with a hearty appetite. She had little time to worry over him: she needed to work.

While she was away in the birthing hut, a trader had come from Fort Pitt with saddlebags full of calico. He had cut off lengths for the seven braves who wanted shirts. Margaret found herself occupied from morning to night, measuring each brave in the manner she had perfected, then cutting out the shirt according to her established pattern and stitching it up. She was paid three shillings for each completed shirt, which greatly benefited Little Mouse and her family when the trader came again. Only once, when in her haste she had sewn a sleeve too close to the selvage, the sleeve had ripped when the brave was hunting and he came to demand his payment returned. He was very angry and Margaret feared the worst, but White Bark came to intervene and the brave relented when she promised to resew the seam with greater care. To her great relief, he did not spread the news of her mistake around the village, which would have harmed her reputation for performing good work.

This was the beginning of Margaret's closer association with White Bark. At first, resisting the notion that he was her father, Margaret had avoided him, but now she recognized his usefulness. He spoke a fair amount of English and had a kingly way about him

Margaret could not help admiring. It was different with his son, Margaret's brother. He preserved his granite way.

A week after White Bark's intervention on her behalf, Margaret went boldly to ask him a question. She found him seated beside his fire. He waved her to a place across from him.

Margaret began at once. "I have been afraid for a long time that I might be forced into a marriage. Girty warned me of that at the start of my stay here." She was careful not to call it her captivity.

White Bark stared at her. "No, my daughter. That is not the Shawnee way."

She carefully concealed her relief.

"Perhaps the women have been tormenting you with this idea," White Bark went on. "Sometimes they are cruel to women captives."

"They have been very kind to me," Margaret told him. "Especially my mother, Little Mouse." It was the first time she had called her that.

"Very well," White Bark said, dismissing her.

After that Margaret went from time to time to his lodge, nearly convinced that White Bark had no ill intentions toward her. She learned that there were certain questions he would not answer, such as whether war was about to break out, as was rumored around the village. He turned his head away when she asked for information he did not wish to give her and smoked as though she had disappeared. At that sign she always made her departure, careful not to strain the fragile alliance by persistence.

As she grew to know him better, she surmised that White Bark was probably younger than her real father had been when he died, but much worn by warfare. He had been gruesomely wounded at the Battle of Point Pleasant with a shot to the hip that had nearly crippled him. Little Mouse called it Lord Dunmore's War, but as Margaret increased her command of the Shawnee language, she learned that most of the tribe, many of whom had fought there, called it the Battle of Point Pleasant, on the Ohio. No one knew the number of losses since the Shawnee carried their wounded and dead away and were not in the habit of counting them. But the cost had been high on both sides, with the pressing possibility of more battles to come.

White Bark no longer hunted with the other braves, and the hours he spent alone in his lodge seemed to have led him to cogitating. On a bright morning in October, Margaret was summoned and found the old chief sitting by his fire.

Gesturing urgently, he asked her why when the sun came up in the east and set in the west he had never been able to see it traveling back and forth. Since the Earth was flat, did she believe that the sun dove under it at night, coming up on the other side in the morning?

To answer him, Margaret balled up the partially finished shirt she had been sewing and placed the ball close to the fire. She pointed out that the flame brightened the near side of the ball, as the sun brightened the east side of Earth in the morning, leaving the other side, which stood for night, in darkness. White Bark seemed satisfied, although her demonstration did not explain where the sun went when it disappeared. She was content to allow him to continue to believe that it passed under the Earth.

⚒️

Fall turned into winter, the second of Margaret's captivity, with little more of consequence. John was thriving. There was always a woman to pass him to when she went to Blue Jacket's house to teach his sons. Both boys now knew their alphabet and were advancing to spelling *apple, bear,* and *deer,* although *cat* was out since they knew no cats and *coyote* was too long. Their white mother tolerated Margaret because she was teaching the two boys to read and write, but she did not become a friend. Margaret wondered at this; the Shawnee women were warmer.

She noticed a drawing in of the tribe as her second winter waned. After the warriors came back from a raid on the Kentucky settlements, a council was held in White Bark's lodge. To Margaret's astonishment, Little Mouse and six of the other older kweewe attended. When Margaret passed, she heard the women speaking; her knowledge of the language was now fully developed and she understood that they were advancing the cause of peace.

Over the three days of the council, the warriors resisted the women's pleading. Long Knife Clark had burned two more Shawnee villages, killing many, and Major William Crawford had just attacked the village of Seekunk, destroying it as well.

"Will there be war?" she asked Robert Dean when he came by to collect a shirt she had sewn.

He shrugged. "The squaws are the peace arguers," he told her. "They fear losses greater than what the tribe suffered at Point Pleasant. Clark is a fierce warrior."

"Who is this Clark?"

"A white captain who crossed the Ohio at Corn Island with a small force some weeks ago. Our runners spread the news, and the braves have been determining how to force him back to the other side of the river. Already he has burned three more of our towns."

The restlessness of the village increased in the early spring, with many braves coming in from raiding, creating a stirring Margaret had not felt before. She began to fear danger not only for herself and for John, but for the whole tribe. The war might break out close by. Months passed with more rumors but nothing happened.

One afternoon when she was grinding corn for winter storage, a white man appeared, led by Little Mouse. Margaret got up, understanding that he might have a message for her, even news of a rescue party on its way.

"What is your name?" she asked, gathering herself.

"Thomas McGuire," he answered. He was about twenty-five and of the fair, blue-eyed tribe, like most of the inhabitants of the Greenbrier Settlement.

"Do you come from the Greenbrier?" she asked.

"No, from Fort Harrod. Six days hard travel. I bring a message."

"What is it?" she asked, trying to see something, a glint of hope or comfort, but his face was as bland as unbaked bread.

"Your husband John Paulee is dead," he told her pompously, "dead many months." He was watching her as though expecting tears or screaming.

Margaret said, "I feared as much. He was grievously wounded when we were taken captive." She remembered how John had run away, holding his side, from which blood was streaming, and how the Shawnee had watched in astonishment, expecting him to fall.

"He died the next day after your capture, at a settler's cabin." McGuire said in an ordinary voice, as though her composure had calmed him, and Margaret understood that he had dreaded her reaction to his news.

"Then why," she asked sternly, "in all this time has no one come to ransom me?"

Tom looked discomfited. "I do not know," he said.

"You must tell me," Margaret said with the voice she used when she was correcting Blue Jacket's little boys. "I must know."

After some hesitation, Tom said that it was believed at the Greenbrier that she had been adopted into the tribe as a wife and had birthed a son.

"My boy is my husband's child!" Margaret cried. "I have suffered no indignity here! I am White Bark's daughter. I am not his concubine!" She spoke with a pride in the distinction she knew at once she should have muffled.

Tom took a step back. "I have only told you what I have heard," he said, and hastened on to give her news of her sister. Agatha had married the son of the governor of Detroit and was with child. "A worthy match," Tom added.

With both hands, Margaret dismissed him. He hurried away, relieved to be gone.

Margaret sat down and returned to her sewing. She felt a hollowness, as though something whose presence she had barely noticed had been stripped away. Now she knew there might be no ransom, she had to admit to herself that she felt great sadness, but in addition, a sort of relief.

The tears she had thought she would shed at the thought of never seeing her mother again, or her brothers and sisters, refused to come, although she sat for a while waiting for them. Were her ties of affection to her family so frail, so easily frayed? She did not know, she did not understand. Something weightier had come between her and those feelings, a weight made up of the orderliness of the life that now included her, a sense of connection she had never experienced before.

It was not that the tribe honored her. They honored only their warriors and the medicine man and woman and, at times, their ancestors. But the tribe had given her a place in their midst, as White Bark's daughter, a place that felt more secure than any she had known before. At the Greenbrier, she had been one among many, a daughter, then a wife, and had she returned there as a widow, she would have needed to struggle to survive. Here, that would not be likely to happen. And John, toddling around the village and chattering his first words of Shawnee, was accepted and indulged as a Shawnee boy. She had never seen a white child so loved or so happy.

With a start, she recalled the news of her sister's marriage in Detroit. By now her first child might already have been born. The news had made little impression; Agatha belonged to a time that now seemed long gone by. Margaret was shocked to discover that her affection for her sister had faded and surmised that her love for her other relatives was also sinking into the past.

Around her, she heard the usual sounds of the village: wood being chopped, a knife sharpened on a flintstone, low talk among the kweewe. She breathed the rich savor of a deer haunch grilled over a fire and felt for the first time the terror of familiarity. No one from her earlier life would believe that familiarity possible for her here. Her ease was a betrayal of her family and her friends, and although they were far away, they must have sensed it. They had abandoned her.

⫷⫷⫸⫷◈⫸⫸⫸

Early the next morning, so early the halfmoon still hung in the sky, the village was stirring. A runner had come in during the night with the news that Clark and his Long Knives had approached within a mile of the village under cover of darkness.

At once preparations for battle began. Margaret gathered with the other women in the center of the village as the horses were driven in and saddled. Then, a long wail on a horn announced the start of drumming. A conch shell blew a piercing note. A whistle pierced the drumming, harsh and high, as White Bark rode into the center of the space, his face fully painted under his eagle feather head dress. He wore a white breast plate made of lengths of bone, and his ceremonial robe fell over his moccasins nearly to the ground.

His warriors began a strange stomping, stooping dance to the pounding of the drums, circling first to the left and then to the right as the strange high whistle pierced the air. As the sun rose, Margaret saw that each warrior was painted in red, black, and white, wearing only a breechcloth and carrying a bow, a fletch of arrows, and a flintlock. When the drumming stopped, they mounted their horses and rode past White Bark at a slow gait. He made no sign of recognition or blessing, but Margaret felt that something potent was passing between him and the younger men. She trembled, realizing that some of these men would not return.

The warriors galloped out of the village.

"Where are they going?" Margaret asked the woman standing beside her, in Shawnee.

Without answering, she hurried Margaret to where the other women were snatching up bits of deer jerky and roasted potatoes still hot from the fire, stuffing their pouches before gathering blankets and children and fleeing into the woods. They were led by an old man who appeared to be too ancient to join the warriors.

Margaret screamed for John, who came running with the other boys. They were carried along with the women like sticks on a flooding river. The old man led the way across ravines and through bramble thickets to a space inside a grove of chestnuts, where they settled on the ground.

Within minutes Margaret heard the war hoop and the pounding of hooves passing close by on the other side of the trees. She laid her hand over John's mouth and crouched down with him inside her shawl. If they were discovered, she thought their white skin might save them, but if there were men from the Greenbrier Settlement with Clark, as well there might be, men who believed the worst of her and had already abandoned her, why would they care if she and her son lived or died?

John soon became restless and strove to push away her hand, and she remembered the captivity doll she'd seen in a cabin at home with its skirt of rags and white featureless face, topped by a bonnet. It was taken down from a hiding place and used to keep a child quiet during a raid. There was no such doll here. She pressed her hand firmly over John's mouth.

Presently the uproar of battle turned and the warriors passed so close Margaret caught a flash of red between the tall guardian trees. She stretched herself flat on the ground, holding John pinned beneath her shoulder. The clamor circled them and then moved off. A little later, one of the kweewe raised her head and, crying softly, gestured toward plumes of black smoke rising above the trees.

All morning, the pillars of smoke rose higher, then spread into the depths of the blue sky. The little group sat and watched in silence with an equanimity that proved they had seen their village burned before.

Around noon, the old man who had led them from the village went out to assess the situation. When he came back, he motioned to the women and children to follow him. No matter what he had seen, his face told Margaret nothing and no questions were asked. Holding John's hand, she followed with the rest.

At the lip of a rise, they stopped. Below them, their village was entirely laid waste. The long houses had crumbled into heaps of smoldering logs, and rugs, baskets, weapons, and food were all buried beneath the ashes. Close by, wounded warriors lay side by side. Among them Margaret recognized Blue Jacket's nephew.

Some of the women, recognizing husbands, brothers, or sons, rushed forward with their strange quavering cry to tip water from their canteens into dry mouths or attempt to lave wounds. Margaret went up to Blue Jacket's nephew, but as she lowered her canteen he croaked his death song and returned to the other side.

Then it was time to attend to the dead. The kweewe washed blood off the bodies while two warriors dug holes as deep as possible in the dry rocky dirt. Each of the dead was blessed by Te-Cu-Sah, the medicine man, and laid in his grave, which the women then filled, stacking stones on top to keep off the wolves. Although they knew they were in constant danger of a new attack, the work was done without hurrying, and again Margaret felt the nameless pull of the connection that now bound her to these strange people.

Te-Cu-Sah then sent the women to gather whatever bits of food had escaped the fire. The sum was hardly enough to fill a saddlebag. Then they set off, led by White Bark and the other surviving braves. It looked, Margaret thought, as though half of their men had perished.

Sleeping on the ground that damp night, Margaret fell into a teeth-chattering chill. She wrapped John in her blanket and nestled next to him, hoping the small heat of her body might warm him.

He came through the night with no apparent harm, but Margaret woke with a fever and the aching limbs of ague.

At dawn, Little Mouse scooped John up and carried him away to feed him a little gruel and care for him. Margaret was left to tend to her own misery as best she could. For five days in their temporary camp, she burned with fever, sipping the acrid dark brown teas Little Mouse brought her. Gradually her fever and chills abated and by the sixth day she and all the rest who had fallen ill that cold night were well enough to travel.

But Margaret was still weak when White Bark gave the order to move on. Little Mouse helped her to mount and then took charge of John, carrying him in front of her on her horse. As they rode out, Margaret had to hold to her saddle horn with one hand for fear that jolting over the rough trail might topple her. Little Mouse rode beside her when the trail was wide enough. John slept throughout their journey.

As they rode, Margaret understood much of what the kweewe near her were saying. The loss of Shawnee warriors was considerable. The women put that down to the fact that due to the surprise nature of the attack, there had been no time to conduct the requisite ceremonials. Some men had even lain with their wives the night before the battle, a deadly mixing of woman power with the warrior spirit, which had weakened them and caused the great losses.

Three days' journey from their burned village, White Bark chose a spot for their next camp on a bare plateau above the river. Here they settled, and the next morning, the men began to chop wood for the new long houses. Margaret noticed that the work was done without complaint and guessed that these people had seen many of their villages burned and had always fallen to with a will to build them again.

White Bark had chosen the site because of the abundant water and game nearby and so the hunting was good, the best Margaret had seen. The first afternoon, hunters brought in three well-grown female deer as well as six wild turkeys. This was the first time since the Greenbrier that Margaret had plucked, skinned, and gutted one of these wild birds; they were disappointingly scrawny beneath their plumage. But with the addition of the roasted deer, the tribe ate more bountifully than before, and it seemed that the new village might bring them better luck, or at least more food.

It was the first time since her capture more than two years earlier that Margaret had eaten until her belly was full. John had his first meat, gnawing with his five teeth on a wild turkey wing, and Margaret knew that the time of weaning was at hand. His first tooth had already caused her pain. When she asked Little Mouse for help, she gave her a mixture to rub on her nipples. It must have been as bitter as gall, for John, trying to suck, made a horrid face and pushed her breast away. Then he scurried off to play with the other boys.

Margaret played her part in the building of White Bark's lodge, which was to be her new home. She skinned the bark off the limbs the men were bringing into camp, smoothing the rough surfaces with her knife. Meanwhile, the men were digging holes at regular intervals around a level patch to hold eight enormous posts that would support the roof. Margaret noticed that there was no arguing, as the supporting timbers were laced with smaller limbs and twigs; a slight dispute between two elders about who should carve the faces of the gods to be hung on two doorway timbers was quickly resolved when Mary Rabbit suggested that each man carve a face. The fearsome images were duly carved and hung, with a twist of tobacco above each.

Margaret had retained a blanket for a pallet, but all her other belongings—her housewife, her sewing kit, and the two little books—had been left behind at the village and burned. She felt great unease at the thought that she would no longer be able to sew shirts. As for the two books that had been of such importance to her and her sister at the beginning of their travail, she had not looked at them for many months, being both fully occupied and at a greater and greater distance from the life those books represented. And it had been many moons since she had written in the open spaces between the lines in Dr. Franklin's volume.

When John pulled at her blouse for his next feed, she pushed him off and offered him, instead, a spoonful of gruel. Angrily, he shoved the spoon away, and the kweewe nearby laughed. Margaret persisted, and, finally, sorrowfully, he gave in and accepted the wretched substitute, while her breast grew hard and painful. Sensing her trouble, Little Mouse brought her a warm poultice that smelled of dried mint leaves. Margaret was grateful, but her breasts remained painful for four days.

CHAPTER SIXTEEN

A**FTER A HARD WINTER**, the spring of the following year was warm and rainy, and by the first of May, the fields were ready for planting. Little Mouse told Margaret that the waxing moon marked the right time for putting in the seeds of the aboveground crops, such as squash and beans, while corn as well as the root crops would not be planted until the next new moon was on the way to full.

Margaret noticed unusual activity among the kweewe, who were baking a large number of loafs of bread and cutting up the abundant game. The work was divided, with the oldest and most honored directing each operation while the younger women hurried about, obeying. Margaret was set the task of keeping the cooking fires supplied with split wood, leaving her tired by the time the long day was finally over.

The braves went about their less arduous task, clearing a dance ground in the middle of the village without the arguing and swearing she remembered from home—but then, the traders had not visited for some time. If they had come and brought the usual allotment of rum, the braves would have been lying sodden and listless, but when the Spring Bread Dance was being prepared, the traders knew from long habit to stay away. They would not be welcome.

The next morning dawned clear and cool. Margaret was up betimes along with the other women. Four of them went over to the dance ground and Margaret, curious as always, followed, holding John firmly by the hand. He was now walking and running and shouting freely, but the solemnity of the occasion seemed to abash him and he stayed quiet.

Using freshly made twig brooms, the women swept from each side of the cleared ground, all four meeting in the middle. Their moccasins returning to the edges were so lightly placed they hardly left a mark in the swept dirt.

The ceremony began at once and lasted into the night. Every member of the tribe except for Margaret and the smallest children had parts to play.

Margaret did not expect to participate. After all, she was still a white woman, and even after more than two years with the Shawnee, some still regarded her with silent suspicion.

She was allowed to watch the kweewe of her lodge robing themselves with bright-colored skirts, shawls, and heavy silver ornaments, drawn from a large trunk. Women, when together, were usually laughing and chattering, but this robing was completed in silence.

Their hair ornaments, Margaret saw, were unusual and even beautiful when attached to their knotted-up glossy black hair, washed earlier that morning in the river with a jimson root mixture and dried in the sun. The top part of each hair ornament was made up of two beaded triangles, white on a ground of black, joined together and attached to ribbons that ran to the hems of their long skirts.

As the decked-out women took their positions in a long line on the east side of the dancing ground, Little Mouse plucked at Margaret's sleeve and pointed her to the end of the line. Margaret protested; she was not ceremonially dressed, but Little Mouse pushed her to her allotted place. To calm her anxiety, Margaret reminded herself that Little Mouse held unimpeachable authority.

Now Margaret's task was to watch and copy the other dancers. The big drum began and the men, bravely painted in red, white, and black above their breech cloths and beaded leggings, formed a line on the west facing the women. The men wore the silver nose rings Margaret saw every day but also long earbobs stretching their lobes nearly to their shoulders and curious turban-like head-dresses, each sprouting five feathers.

The dances were simpler than the square dances Margaret remembered from the Greenbrier. It was just a step-pat left followed by a step-pat right, the men dancing the same pattern as the women, coming a little forward and then going back with each repetition. All the dancers wore the same expression of quiet absorption, their eyes fixed on the ground.

After about thirty minutes the drumming stopped and the two lines fell apart, but not for long. Soon, as the insistent drum began again, the two lines reformed and the monotonous step-pat, step-pat recommenced.

By midafternoon, when a break came with plentiful loaves of bread and roasted deer, John had wandered off, taken over by a group of children who kept him quiet. Margaret longed to use him as an excuse to retreat, but she was no longer nursing him and she knew she would not be liberated from the evening dances. They began as soon as the sun had set and continued without intermission until the first glimmerings of dawn. Then she finally fell onto her pallet in her lodge, hearing the footsteps of the other dancers, dispersing in silence.

Next morning, she was rousted early to help with the spring planting. She spent the next three days digging holes and dropping in corn kernels, sealed with a sliver of the fish the men had brought up from the river. Tamping dirt into each hole, she felt the ache in her back almost as a benediction, proof that her labor, willingly given, had perhaps brought her closer to the complete acceptance for which she had begun to long. She had absorbed the Shawnee language as though through her skin, and Little Mouse and the other older kweewe now talked freely with her and included her in their games as well as their work. But the younger women still maintained a silence Margaret knew was not friendly. As for the braves, they ignored her, to her relief.

The following morning, two little white boys arrived in the village, taken during Uncle's raid: Jackie Calloway, about nine years old, Margaret guessed, and Dicky Hou, about twelve. They were placed in Margaret's care, to John's great delight, and would have found welcome in White Bark's lodge if he had not been bitterly distracted by the death of his son, Margaret's brother, in the latest raid. Margaret hoped that the two lively boys might begin to assuage his grief, but it was not to be. He ignored them as he had begun to ignore her.

For three long days and nights, White Bark was inconsolable, tearing his hair and smearing his body with mud, refusing food, water, and sleep. All night Margaret heard his groans. The ceremonial dances that were meant to sanctify his son's death did nothing to relieve him. Then, as Margaret listened at the edge of the lodge, keeping her new charges and John quiet and close to her side, she heard that White Bark was forming a plan. Suddenly calm, he called in his braves and told them of his decision:

according to sacred tradition, everything that had belonged to his son must be destroyed.

Margaret did not at first understand her danger since, she believed, she belonged to White Bark as daughter and not to his son as sister. But a day later as she passed the blacksmith's shed, she heard a white trader ask who was to be burned. The blacksmith pointed in silence at her.

As she hurried away, she tried to reassure herself by remembering White Bark's evident partiality, but then she discerned that, as his dead son's sister, she might now be considered to have belonged to him along with his weapons, his buffalo robes, and all his other plunder. To know the worst as soon as possible, she began to prowl around the council house, overhearing arguing about her fate that went on for two days and nights. She could not understand every word, but the passion of their disagreements was unmistakable and she knew she was in grave danger.

In council, many of the Shawnee argued for her life as an adopted daughter of the tribe but others, following the tradition, insisted on her destruction. They had already burned all the young warrior's possessions in a great bonfire and shot his horses, too. Now only Margaret remained.

At the end of the second day when no agreement had been reached, the white man Alexander McKee was sent for to settle the dispute, which gave Margaret some reason to hope. She had heard McKee spoken of respectfully around the camp because he was the son of a Shawnee woman, Margaret Tecumsah Opessea, who had taught him to know and honor the tribe's ways. Although a British agent, he had often pleaded the tribe's case in disputes with the British, and in return they had given him the title of Great

White Elk. Because he was half white, Margaret hoped that his ties to the tribe would not count for more than her life.

McKee sent word that he would not tolerate her burning, but he himself did not appear.

After overhearing the third night of fierce arguing, which did not reach a resolution, Margaret was beginning to imagine stealing away.

Nearly all the tribes of the Shawnee had sent members to the council; their meetings lasted until the fourth day. Margaret, trembling with terror, made darting trips to the edge of the council house and heard White Bark describe the details of her burning and where it would take place. She knew it would mean a slow fire and hours of agony when her courage would crumple and she would scream, plead, and cry, destroying her honor even as she died.

On the fourth morning, a second message was brought from McKee by an interpreter, warning of serious retaliation if Margaret was burned. The interpreter, Samuel Flint, a large bearded white man, spent the day arguing with the elders and rallying those who objected to Margaret's killing. By the afternoon, she thought she was beginning to hear a modulation in White Bark's tone, as though he had begun to question his own wisdom. At last White Bark pointed to the handsomely mounted flintlock that Flint carried and announced that he would accept it in exchange for Margaret's life.

With a flourish, Flint handed White Bark his weapon.

The gift achieved what no amount of arguing had been able to accomplish. The incident was never mentioned again, and Margaret to her astonishment was treated with the same consideration as before by her adoptive father.

But she had learned that his kindness was no guarantee, and the barbarism of his ways assaulted her with new and unexpected force. And when she tried to thank Samuel Flint for saving her life, he waved her away scornfully.

As the days warmed, she occupied herself with caring for little Jackie Calloway, who was formally adopted by the tribe. To her sorrow, Dicky Hou was taken away and she was never able to discover his fate. The disappearance of his comrade in misfortune deeply trouble Jackie and for many nights he woke screaming. He had seen his parents slaughtered before he was abducted, and Margaret could not persuade him that he was safe. She spent one night rocking him in her arms—he was as thin as a stick and she feared fever and ague—but the next morning, he woke with clear eyes and calmly asked her to promise once more that he would not be taken away. After she had given him her word, he was finally reassured and the nightmares ceased.

That winter Jackie was included in the life of John and the other Shawnee boys, dressed as they were in deerskin tunic, breech cloth, and leggings. Every morning, he went down to the banks of the river and plunged in with the other boys. When he came back to the lodge, he was shaking with cold, his hair frozen on his head. Margaret always built up the fire before he returned and wrapped him in a blanket. Because he was so thin, she feared that the arduous custom would lead to his falling ill, but to her surprise, he began to gain flesh and muscle and by spring was as sturdy as the other boys, speaking Shawnee and dressed as they were and could only be recognized as white by his blue eyes.

As the summer passed, Margaret could not have explained to herself, let alone to anyone else, why as the end of her third year with the Shawnee was approaching, she found it easier to accept their ways. Meeting the murderer of her daughter on the path to the spring, she saw before she knew his identity a tall upstanding figure, noble in countenance and movement, then remembered with a shudder how he had snatched her infant from her arms and slung her against a tree. She would never forgive him or speak to him readily, but a rising sense she could not suppress of his reason for what had seemed an act of wanton cruelty—the survival of his band, their presence signaled by her baby's wailing—began to weaken and then to dismantle her rage. He, too, had only wanted to live.

She remembered the tale she had heard one evening by the fire. A bear, killed, skinned, and gutted after the proper ceremony had reappeared some time later as a spirit, gleaming through the trees. Perhaps her daughter might return to her some evening as a pale light in the forest.

But then she remembered that her daughter had had no death ceremony.

CHAPTER SEVENTEEN

I N SEPTEMBER, at the start of Margaret's fourth year of captivity, she began to feel a new concern for her son, John. Now a well-grown three-and-a-half-year-old, he prattled in Shawnee rather than in English as he trailed after the older boys, initiated into their games and mimicking their ways. He shared their scorn for the girls and drove them away in spite of Margaret's remonstrances.

That winter, Margaret noticed that, despite his white skin, John wore the facial expressions and carried himself with the pride that marked the Shawnee boys. At the same time, the kweewe lavished him with attention and little treats: a handful of shelled hickory nuts or dried berries. Often, he spent the night in another woman's lodge, snuggled in bear skins with her sons.

This attention seemed likely, Margaret thought, to attach her son to the Shawnees with a bond that might prove impossible to break. She knew that the time might come, even if it was years in the future, when by some strange chance they would be reunited with their white kin. How would John as a Shawnee boy fit in?

In the evening, she drew John into her long house and told him the old tales—the long-haired girl in her tower, the old witch in the woods—forcing him to repeat the English words that were no longer familiar. But it was an awkward exercise; he escaped as soon as he could to run with the other boys until darkness.

━━◀◀◀►◉◄►►►━━

As though to fulfill Margaret's prophesy, a white man from the Greenbrier Settlement named Higgins appeared in the village in early spring and demanded to speak to her. Margaret was called to meet Higgins on the threshold of her lodge. She had been scrubbing dirty garments on the banks of the river and was wet-handed and red-faced with exertion as she approached him.

She was astonished to find much kindly concern on his weathered face. He reached for her wet hands and pressed them warmly. "I bring a message from your mother," he said.

"Is she well?"

"As well as can be expected for a woman of her age. She mourns your absence, Margaret, and prays every day on her knees for your return."

"I am waiting to be ransomed. I have waited more than four years," Margaret told him.

"Surely you had opportunities to flee?"

"At the cost of my life, and of my son's. I do not understand why it has taken so long to bring the money. Do you have it now?" She asked it fearfully.

Higgins hesitated. "We heard some time back that you had married here and bore a child, although your mother refuses to believe it."

Margaret raised her voice. "My son is John Paulee's child! His father was murdered on the trail. I have suffered no indignity here," she insisted. Seeing that Higgins seemed unwilling to believe her, she called John, who was storming an anthill nearby. But when he came, Margaret realized his appearance would not lend credence to her story. "Speak to the gentleman in English," she ordered, but John's words were garbled.

Higgins crouched to examine the little boy, who stared at him fearlessly.

"He has his father's eyes," he said. "I knew him well in the old days. I helped him raise your cabin."

Margaret gasped with relief. She remembered now that Higgins had been an occasional visitor.

Higgins stood up. "I bring an ample ransom, two hundred dollars gathered from your friends at the Greenbrier, but the old chief refuses to accept it."

"I will speak to him," Margaret said. But when she went into the lodge, she found the chief speechless, stretched on a buffalo robe by the fire. Little Mouse, who was standing watch, told her that an evil spirit had attacked him a few minutes before, stretching him nearly lifeless. There was no question of speaking now of her ransom. Margaret ran to dismiss Higgins and then returned to White Bark's side.

Her chief concern at this time was attending to her father, who continued nearly lifeless. His patience in the face of death touched her. She realized that he had in fact become her father.

On the first day, she brought him deer meat and bread and a canteen of water. He ate sparingly, leaning up on his elbow. But on the second day, he refused all food, agreeing only to a few sips of water. On the third day, he refused even water and told Margaret not to disturb him with more offers of sustenance.

After that she could only watch helplessly. He did not seem to be in pain. He did not groan or cry out as his face grew dull and his breath slowed; she knew the end was near. On the third evening, he began to chant in a low quavering voice, ancient words she did not understand. His voice grew stronger as he went on. The whole tribe had gathered, in silence, outside the lodge. John and Jackie kept watch with the others.

At sunrise, White Bark woke Margaret with a word and gestured to her to come nearer. She knelt beside him as he turned his wasted face and began to speak in Shawnee.

"My time is upon me," he said. Pointing to the lodge door opening, he bade Margaret to fix her eyes on a point in the brightening sky, in no way marked out but at a certain distance from the horizon.

"When the sun reaches that point, my spirit will take flight," he told her.

As the rising sun approached the spot, White Bark spoke with great concern for Margaret's situation once he, her protector and father, was gone. He feared that her lodge would not be kept supplied with firewood and that the kweewe would begin to persecute her.

"The women here seem sincerely attached to me," Margaret told him, "and I chop and split my own wood."

As though satisfied, he stretched out and closed his eyes. He did not speak again.

Margaret saw that as the sun mounted the eastern sky, it was moving closer to the spot he had shown her. When it crossed that spot, White Bark signed deeply and left the world.

Outside the lodge, the long ululations of the women's mourning began.

Until that moment, White Bark's friends had stayed outside, as though recognizing and accepting that his white daughter should be given pride of place. But as soon as he expired, a horde of kweewe surged in and Margaret was glad to leave. Her part in White Bark's dying was over.

All that night, the tribe danced. Margaret was excused because she was needed to keep the children away. They were not allowed at death rituals. In spite of John's protests, she was able to persuade him to stay with the other children and was grateful, as she'd been before, for his grudging obedience, learned along with the freedom he so much enjoyed.

The next morning, after the all-night vigil of chanting and dancing, White Bark was laid out in the lodge, clothed in a new deerskin shirt without buttons and the beaded moccasins he had prized. His bow, arrows, and rifle were laid across his chest. Margaret saw that his long hair had been carefully combed and his face painted with red-and-white marks.

His one remaining son, Wa-Pu-Sit-Tu, chose and directed a man and a woman to dig the grave at the edge of the settlement. Margaret, watching, remembered that the Shawnee kept no grave-yards and erected no monuments to their dead, moving on and leaving them behind when the time came, without apparent regrets. She remembered the pitiful cemetery at the Greenbrier, with its spindly wooden crosses that were washed clean of painted names and dates by the first hard rain. Yet relatives still gathered on occasion to lay bunches of wildflowers that withered before the week was out.

Four braves carried the body, wrapped in blankets. Diminished by his illness, White Bark seemed to weigh no more than a dead branch as they laid him carefully in the grave. It was four feet deep, lined with bark. With the tribe watching, the medicine man sang and pounded his drum. Then the earth was shoveled in by the same pair who had dug it out.

Smoke rose from small fires lit around the grave, the smoke pungent with dried herbs. A pair of ravens circled slowly overhead before heading off to the river, and Margaret wondered if they were carrying away her father's soul. Five days of all-night dancing ensued, followed by a feast that brought the funeral rites to a close.

As soon as six days had passed, Higgins reappeared in the village and began to negotiate Margaret's ransom with Wa-Pu-Si-Tu. White Bark's son accepted the two hundred dollars Higgins brought without hesitation, and Margaret began to prepare to leave. Her heart was torn, especially when Little Mouse and the other kweewe who had become her friends came to her, weeping and protesting that she was a daughter of the tribe and had an obligation to stay with them.

They also raised a serious objection to her taking John, insisting that as the only grandson of White Bark, his presence in the village was essential to its survival. Margaret had guessed long since that they believed John was fathered there and she had never tried to argue. Now they regarded John as a pledge that she would return.

"I will never leave my son," Margaret told them. "And I must go." Little Mouse persisted and carried the case to the council. After a long night of deliberation, it was decided that she could take her boy with her. Margaret rejoiced, silently. It would have been cruel to express joy in the face of her friends' distress. But at the root of her joy, she felt a sharp fear of the future opening in front of her

At dark, she put the two boys to bed. Jackie was fearful and restless, and to comfort him she sang one of the old Greenbrier songs she'd learned from her mother: "Go tell Jemima, the old gray goose is dead." Although the words were not particularly reassuring, the soft lilt of the melody had the desired effect. As soon as

Jackie's eyes were closed—John was already fast asleep—Margaret left the lodge and went down to the river.

She sat on the bank, watching the smooth, uninterrupted flow of the dark water. The sky was closed by a thick lid of clouds and she could see no stars. After a while, the lid lifted and the gleam of the new moon shot out and crossed the river almost to her feet. Margaret remembered one of Little Mouse's prophesies: the new moon's path on the water foretold a journey. She tried to feel that she would be journeying home, then felt with dismay that thought of the Greenbrier roused only a dry, thin fondness, as of a doll left out in the rain long ago and forgotten.

She did not feel that she had made the decision to return. Higgins had simply presented the money to her brother and, after having it counted by one of his lieutenants, he had quickly accepted it. During her years in the village he had never spoken to her. Perhaps he had always been waiting for this outcome.

And, of course, in the question of her ransom, her wishes had not been considered; it was not their way. She was not sure in any event what she would have answered if she had been asked whether she wanted to go back.

In the end, the only obstacle had been the kweewes' passionate wish to keep her boy. She knew that if she did not now return home—the word tasted sour in her mouth—there would be no further attempt to ransom her. She would be lost and soon forgotten, except perhaps by her mother, whose heart would break at the news of her betrayal.

Here, John would grow up a Shawnee and a warrior, and in all likelihood be killed in one of their incessant wars. Before she was old, Margaret herself would forget her English as she was woven ever more tightly into this world. It was even possible that she might one day marry and bear many children, replenishing the tribe, as she would be expected to do.

She shuddered as a cool breeze touched her face. Who would she be, no longer a white woman but an adopted outcast, a sort of half-breed? She would remain a stranger even if she chose the tribe in place of her white family.

But what life awaited her back in Virginia? She did not believe she would ever again find her place there, ever be forgiven and absolved. She knew the grudge-bearing propensity of the settlers who looked on any absence, even if unwilled, as a betrayal. She had been gone too long.   Her son seemed an Indian boy. Some of the women in the Greenbrier would always doubt that he had a white father, imagining an unchristian alliance had kept her in the village for four years.

Back with her own people, she and John would always be outcasts.

A little owl called softly in the tree behind her and she tried to remember when she had learned to distinguish owl cries from Shawnee calls. So much of her learning had seemed to be conveyed by the air. The lid closed again over the sky and the moon disappeared, withdrawing its silver trail across the water. Still gripped by uncertainty, Margaret went back to her lodge and tried to sleep.

Early the next morning, Little Mouse summoned Margaret to a meeting of the council. Feeling her powerlessness, Margaret stood in front of the forty men and women assembled there. She saw the faces of many men who had never given her any difficulties, but now they were closed against her. She had come to know the kweewe as they lived and worked together, but she knew she would never be mentioned again after she was gone. Loneliness assailed her.

In Shawnee, the young chief Wa Pu Sit Ta told her that she must pack and prepare to leave at once. Higgins was to take her, gathering other ransomed white women along the way back east to the settlements.

She hurried to her lodge, followed by five kweewe, who were lamenting and weeping. She tried to reassure them that she would return for a visit and bring John, but neither she nor they believed her.

Inside the lodge, she bundled her few possessions into a length of deerskin and slung it over her shoulder. Then she shouted for John, who was playing with the other boys at the edge of the river. He came running, then stared in bewilderment when she told him, "We are going on a journey."

At the door to the cabin, Higgins was waiting for her with the reins of two horses over his arm. He offered to help her up, but she mounted briskly on her own. Higgins handed her John, and she tried to settle him on the saddle in front of her, but he was crying and struggling and she knew she would not be able to hold him. Higgins rode up beside her and took the boy. He wrapped a length of rope around him, lashing him to his saddle, and although the boy continued to struggle, he could not escape. His screams rode with them through the village, where many Shawnee stood silently watching, and out to the edge of the forest.

As they started on the trail through the trees, little Jackie Calloway came tearing after them, shouting, "What shall I do now?" He attempted to run alongside the horses until Higgins threatened him with his whip. He fell back, sobbing, and John strained toward him from Higgins's saddle.

Tears ran down Margaret's cheeks as she turned to wave Jackie back to the village. He had not been ransomed. He belonged to the tribe.

CHAPTER EIGHTEEN

A FTER A DAY'S hard ride through the wilderness, up jagged hills and down rocky ravines, Margaret, John, and Higgins reached the cabin of one Mr. McCormick and found three women, also newly ransomed, housed there. Higgins explained that they were all to pass the winter together, a piece of information he had heretofore withheld. McCormick himself was off hunting in the woods, sore pressed to feed his guests.

Margaret looked with misgivings around the miserable cabin. Mr. McCormick, she was told, was an elderly bachelor, and his cabin displayed the dirt and disorder of a solitary life. Then she scrutinized the three women who were to be her winter companions, standing or sitting in various attitudes that revealed their characters. They were watching her as well, and she took pains to introduce herself, going from one to the other with an outstretched right hand.

The first, a pretty girl although a little worn, seized her hand eagerly. "Lucy Grey," she said. "A war party of Cherokee took me a year ago when I was crossing the mountains."

"Alone?" Margaret asked, surprised.

Before Lucy could answer, a stout middle-aged woman announcing herself as Caroline McDimmit said, "She was a-following after the soldiers."

"I was their cook!" Lucy Grey protested.

A quiet-looking elderly woman intervened. "I'm sure you had good intentions, dear, no matter what the outcome." She took Margaret's hand and squeezed it. "I'm Matilda Gage. They took me when I was digging potatoes outside Fort Harrod. We was starving, somebody had to go. I was not ill-used," she added.

It could be worse, Margaret thought. All three women were used to hardship and they would find ways of getting along.

McCormick came in, a wizened old man sporting a big black beard; he'd found no game. He saluted Higgins, who began at once to count out paper three-pence notes and Spanish dollars into McCormick's hand. Then, without a word of farewell, Higgins turned to leave. Catching hold of his sleeve, Margaret asked, "Is it not possible to proceed directly to the Greenbrier?"

"Winter will soon close the mountains to all passage," Higgins told her. "You and your boy will be safe here till the weather breaks." John, clinging to his mother's skirt, let out a howl.

During the three dreary months that followed, Margaret's principal task was attempting to comfort John, who cried day and night to be returned to the Shawnee. Margaret used her whole store of songs as she rocked him in her arms, but even "Go tell it on the mountain" which had been his favorite had lost its appeal. She had little to promise him, especially as the wretched place reminded her too keenly of the cabins "at home".

Mr. McCormick was no company. He lay insensible with drink from sunset to noon, and only when Margaret prodded him could he be persuaded to go out, grumbling, and shoot a wild turkey. He expected the women to do all his chores in repayment for his scant hospitality. They took turns drawing water from the spring a league away, carrying two buckets back to the cabin slung from an ox bow Margaret found in the shed.

McCormick lay snoring when the wood pile gave out, and since the other women had never handled an ax, Margaret was elected to split firewood until her palms were raw. As for the out-house, all refused to consider it, and complaints rose in a chorus the first cold winter night when they were forced to make use of the malodorous shack. Margaret had exiled the chamber pot to the shed to end the arguments about who was to empty it. She set an example, she hoped, by parading to the outhouse no matter the foulness of the weather.

On the third day of this new captivity (for Mr. McCormick did not allow the women to venture outside the dooryard except to fetch water or use the outhouse), Margaret began to work to persuade the other women to help her clean the cabin. "None of us, I believe," she said, although she had scant evidence, "is used to living in a pigsty. We are here willy-nilly until spring, and the time will pass easier in a more orderly place."

Matilda Gage agreed to make use of the broom. She came, Margaret surmised, from gentle folk and had some book learning. She spoke clearly and calmly, with a soft accent that reminded Margaret of home. After sweeping for a while, she leaned on her broom, objecting that cleaning the cabin was a labor worthy of Hercules, who had shoveled out the Augean stables in ancient Greek times. It was an apt comparison since on the last cold night, Mr. McCormick had brought his horse inside to spare its freezing. He did not offer the same hospitality to the women's horses; they had to make the best of it in the shed and grew thick fur as a consequence.

Margaret was able to convince Caroline that scrubbing Mr. McCormick's filthy tinware would spare them diseases, and she finally agreed to take on the task. "I will be a model to the others," she said.

Lucy Grey, a saucy wench, refused to rise from her pallet to help with the sweeping, scouring, and scrubbing. After conferring with Matilda and Caroline, Margaret approached the girl to announce that those who would not work, would not eat. Lucy, who was possessed of a healthy appetite, sprang up at once, seized the broom, and soon sent dust particles dancing in a ray of sunlight that penetrated the filthy windows. Mr. McCormick meanwhile sat spraddled on a sawhorse and laughed at the women's activity.

After two days of labor, the puncheon floor was nearly white, the moth-eaten buffalo robes beaten, the pallets aired (Margaret was sure many unclean bodies had rested on them), and the big iron kettle scrubbed, filled from the spring and set outdoors over a good fire to prepare for making soap. Mr. McCormick rose from his sawhorse to supervise the soap making, blaming the condition of his cabin on the lack.

"There is always hot water," Margaret said with asperity, using both hands to thrust him away. He had the unpleasant habit of standing far too close when he addressed her. Rebuffed, he turned his attention to Lucy, who repelled him with a blow to the jaw that rang through the cabin, following it with a kick to his fundament as he turned away, bellowing with pain. "Show me your silver first!" she shouted, knowing the man had none.

McCormick knew better, Margaret noticed, than to approach Matilda Gage, who managed to retain a certain rustic elegance even in those surroundings. She took to tying on her worn lace cap every morning over her freshly braided hair, as though she was on her way to meeting. Margaret admired the way her dignity protected her.

As for Caroline McDimitt, her size was her protection. She was a sturdy, well-rounded woman who had managed to maintain her girth even in captivity. Before Margaret asked her, she turned to the work with a will, carrying all the bedding out into the sun and beating it with a stout stick.

That evening they sat down at a scrubbed table to pick to pieces and devour two rabbits McCormick had brought in. He kept the third rabbit for himself.

By the time the worst of the winter was over and the snow and ice had begun to melt, John finally stopped begging to return to the Shawnee. He became very quiet and pale, and Margaret feared for his health. She brewed toddies for him with the hoarhound root she had learned to dig beneath the snow, adding a teaspoon of treacle, but he did not regain his color or his appetite.

On a day of warming sun, Mr. McCormick without asking for permission took John along when he went after deer, and Margaret heard the boy's loud clear laughter as he came back, riding behind McCormick and holding on with both arms. After that he trailed after their host all day long and began to regain his appetite.

Now, with the longer days and increasing warmth, Margaret began to plead with Mr. McCormick to start on the journey east. He did not favor leaving yet—there might still be a late snow in the mountains—and Margaret surmised that he did not want to leave at all. The company of the four women was pleasant, his food was prepared with care, his cabin scoured every week, and his shirt and trousers boiled in the soap kettle to rid them of fleas. During the laundering process, he lounged in a long garment Margaret recognized as a flannel dressing gown. Why should he undertake the rigors of the trail? After all, he had already been paid.

She surmised from the lengthening days that they had entered the month of April and again approached McCormick to persuade him to start out. "We must wait out blackberry winter," he told her, reclining at his ease on his pallet. "Feed the horses a few handfuls of the remaining corn," a task Margaret assigned to Caroline. And indeed, a rush of cold weather froze the melting snow around the cabin and for five days more they were marooned, McCormick explaining that riding through ice would slit the horses' fetlocks.

"What is the meaning of this cold?" Matilda asked, trying for common ground.

"It sets the blackberries for next summer's harvest," he told her.

"I remember hearing that same reason given at the Greenbrier," Margaret told her.

Warm weather returned on the sixth day. Lucy was all for the women starting out at once on their own—she was devoured by restlessness—but Margaret reminded her, "We scarcely know in what direction to start."

Overhearing, McCormick heaved a big laugh. "I have made the journey three times with other ransomed women, more patient and grateful than you have proved to be. You'd scarcely survive, lost in the mountains."

Now Matilda Gage began to pray morning and evening for their deliverance; morning had been sufficient before, and even Caroline, who had been so staunch, began to sink into despair. "I will never see my children again," she said.

McCormick seemed to be moved by her desperation. That evening he began to make preparations, packing saddlebags with blankets, canteens of water, strips of deer jerky and strings of dried apples, as well as bags of ground cornmeal.

"Surely we will not need so much," Margaret objected, but McCormick only grunted. Then she admitted to herself that she had little idea of the length of their journey. From her nine days ride after her capture to the first Shawnee camp and then the two removals from villages due to warfare, she had lost track of the distance that lay between her and what she still deemed civilization, although now she knew it needed another name.

That was the first night McCormick left the rum jug plugged. Next morning, he rousted the four women out of their blankets before first light, advising them to lay on every garment they had (which were few) for the ride ahead. He told Margaret that 'twas better for John to ride on the saddle behind him, and the little boy was delighted, clasping the big man with both arms as Margaret wedged him into the saddle.

The wilderness they broke through that first day extended without change for the thirteen days that followed. There were no trails. Here and there a faint track, made by deer, relieved them for a while, but they were soon back in nearly impenetrable brush.

They rode slowly. Their way was often barred by fallen trees or thickets too dense to penetrate, necessitating a detour. Mr. McCormick seemed certain of their way and sang or whistled as they jogged slowly along, single file. Accepting his guidance, Margaret even began to like him a little.

Every night, they stopped at dusk near a half-frozen stream or sometimes by a settler's field of corn, abandoned when he fled back East. The winter-dried ears were poor fodder for the horses but they chomped them eagerly. Even long boiling over the camp fire did not make them soft enough for humans. They shared deer jerky and dried apples and spooned up a gruel made with corn meal and hot water.

But the supplies that had seemed too ample at first dwindled at a perilous rate; the women were always ravenous for their one meal of the day, and Mr. McCormick, who had a huge appetite, refused all notion of rationing. "Fill your bellies," he advised. "We'll find settlers to feed us by and by." He also promised to bring in game but he was no kind of shot, and day after day he brought back nothing, cursing as he came out of the woods that the savages had taken everything.

"They have names," Margaret protested. "Do you not know them?"

"No need," McCormick said grimly.

To spite him, Margaret began to list all the names she had learned, beginning with the ones she had imagined during those first days on the trail, names that seemed ridiculous to her now: Topknot, Uncle, Brother One, Brother Two, Raven Wing, then proceeding to the names she had learned, Shawnee now nearly as comfortable in her mouth as English. But John, overhearing, began to wail and Margaret stopped to comfort him.

On the fourteenth day, their provisions were exhausted and soon hunger assailed them. Margaret urged the women to fill themselves with water, but that caused too many stops for relief along the trail and McCormick forbade it.

John was fading rapidly. He no longer had the strength to hold on to Mr. McCormick as he rode, and Margaret took him back in front of her on her saddle and held him tightly with one arm. She felt a desperation so keen she nearly cried out. Was she condemned to lose her second child?

It was in that extremity that she spied a hawk as they were breaking camp on the fifteenth morning. It was sitting on the top branch of a big bare maple, tearing at a pheasant it held in its claws. Margaret, riding ahead, had seen it. She did not dare to alert the others for fear of driving the hawk away with its prey. Slipping from her saddle, she found a round smooth stone and launched it with all her strength. The stone struck the hawk in the breast and, startled, it dropped the pheasant in the branches and flew off.

"Help me," Margaret called as the others rode up.

It fell to Lucy as the youngest and nimblest to climb the maple, free the pheasant from the branches, and bring it down. Margaret snatched the bird and laid it out on a stump, then swiftly plucked and gutted it while the others stood watching, Matilda Gage weeping with hunger.

Then she spitted the bird on a stick and held it over a small fire, turning it as a few drops of grease sputtered on the coals. When it was partly cooked and the delicious aroma rose, she shoved off the other women, tore out a wad of bloody breast meat, and chewed it before pushing it into John's limp mouth. He gagged. She stroked his throat. Finally, he swallowed.

"Have at it," she told the others and they tore at the bird with their bare hands. Only McCormick held back, laughing at the spectacle as he lit and smoked his hunger-killing pipe.

After that, providence seemed to take mercy on the little caravan. The country slowly became more open as they rode southeast, the way a little easier, although by now Lucy and Matilda were groaning from saddle sores rubbed raw. Indeed, the horses endured the ordeal with less trouble than their riders, although Margaret's Jenny was going lame.

CHAPTER NINETEEN

O N THE MORNING of the sixteenth day, Fort Pitt appeared between the trees with a grandeur and solemnity Margaret had not expected, since she had never seen the stout stockades erected in Kentucky. As they rode closer, with McCormick hallooing and waving his hat at the sentries, she saw that it was only a worn wooden palisade, surmounted by two watch towers. McCormick was recognized as he rode ahead, and the great timber gates swung open, creaking loudly.

The women rode in behind him. When they had dismounted, women and children clustered around them, asking where they came from and for what purpose. McCormick interrupted before Margaret could reply. "I have rescued these women from the Indians. They have suffered grievously. Pray make them welcome."

The crowd fell away with awed looks and they were beckoned to an enormous iron pot of deer meat stew, bubbling over the big cook fire in the center of the fort.

Margaret heard a woman shouting and turned to see her sister Agatha rushing toward her with outstretched arms. They embraced each other fiercely, both sobbing. Margaret made haste to introduce John, who, dirty and in rags, looked up at his aunt in bewilderment. Agatha pulled back, studying him.

"Whose child is this?" she asked.

"Mine, and John Paulee's."

"But surely you were not with child when we were captured."

"I did not know it yet," Margaret told her, "but it was soon apparent. John was born eight months later."

"But with all the trials you endured, surely you would have miscarried—"

"Enough, Sister," Margaret interrupted. "Believe me or not as you wish, it is no concern of mine. And I see you are with child," she added.

Agatha patted her belly. "I was married Christmas a year ago. My husband is Captain Michael Randolf. He is the Detroit governor's son. He is away subduing another savage village or you would make his acquaintance and know him for a gentleman."

"I am glad you are well placed," Margaret replied with circumspection. "Does our mother know?"

"Certainly. Captain Randolf sent a runner to the Greenbrier with the news. Mother wept with satisfaction. But she is disconsolate over your fate, Margaret."

"She does not know my fate. Perhaps she has swallowed rumors."

Agatha did not answer. She spooned a hearty portion of deer stew onto a tin plate and handed it to Margaret. "We heard you were starving."

"No. The hunting was good until the last few days, and we were well fed."

"But surely as a captive—"

"Enough, Sister." Margaret said. She thought with sorrow that Agatha might never understand the way her life during the past four years had defied expectations.

Then Margaret followed her sister into a pleasant house

situated on what passed for a main street. Boards were laid in the street over muddy patches so that women could pass without dirtying their skirts. Agatha served her a cup of India tea from a china teapot and fell to chattering about her husband's prospects of following his father as governor of Detroit. Margaret felt a space opening between them; Agatha seemed to have forgotten their time together in the wilderness.

That evening the cook of the garrison prepared a grand feast: two wild turkeys, stuffed with winter onions and sweet potatoes and roasted whole in tin campfire ovens, with hominy and baked squash and dried apples. There was even a flagon of aged cider, with a sting to it. Margaret sat at table beside her sister, flanked by the militia officers, but there was little talk. Agatha's distrust had chilled the air, or else it was the effect of scurrilous rumors. She saw some of the men glancing curiously at John.

The colonel in charge of the fort insisted that all five wayfarers bed down for the night in his parlor and ordered his black slave to spread feather beds on the floor. Margaret tried to settle herself with John in the crook of her arm, but she felt nearly suffocated by the feathers and soon rolled out to sleep on the bare floor. She had not expected that four years of sleeping on dirt would make such softness intolerable to her.

McCormick woke Margaret and the others before dawn, ordering them to saddle up. Their provisions and water had been renewed. Agatha was still asleep in a bedroom upstairs and Margaret did not wake her.

As they rode out through the fort's gates, Margaret asked McCormick, "How many more days?" But he shrugged and refused to answer.

She soon realized that the worst of the journey was before them.

Fort Pitt stood at the confluence of two rivers and as they rode away, McCormick announced, "The Monongahela and the Allegany," with a wave of his arm.

"*Land*, what kind of a name is that?" Lucy asked, kicking her sorrel to ride up beside McCormick, who smiled down at her.

Margaret noticed that something was building between the two. "I believe Monongahela is an Indian name," she said, riding up alongside them and speaking with a crispness that surprised her.

"People hereabouts call it the Mon," McCormick corrected her.

The three of them rode along in a tight knot until a bramble thicket separated them. Then they continued single file, breaking into a trot as McCormick rode forward. Only Caroline, possessed of greater wisdom, Margaret thought, kept to a walk behind them. All of the horses were saddle-sore now and overused, which did not prevent McCormick from urging them along at a trot.

As the day progressed, Margaret was fully occupied with threading her way through a forest so dense that twigs slapped and scratched her face. John, secure behind McCormick's broad back, twittered and laughed until at last he fell asleep, rocked by the old gelding's motion. Meanwhile, Margaret's Jenny, dulled to passivity by little feed and long days on the trail, still jerked her head in protest as twigs scraped her eyes. The other riders were equally occupied; even Lucy fell silent as the horses plunged down a gorge so steep they slid in the mud on their haunches. Lucy gave a little scream and Matilda gasped as Margaret fixed her eyes on her son who in sleep was listing sideways on McCormick's back.

McCormick abruptly called a stop on the edge of the creek

that threaded the ravine. They slid from their saddles to sip water and chew hard tack the fort had provided.

Mounted again, they struggled up the east side of the ravine. The horses slid on stones, snorted, tossed their heads, balked, and had to be whipped onward. In the heat of their struggle, Margaret saw McCormick, ahead of them on the ridge, rein in and look back with a concern she had not expected. "Courage, ladies," he shouted, using a term he had never employed before. As though the word freshened their spirits, Margaret, Caroline, Lucy, and Matilda assaulted the last rise with renewed vigor.

It did not last. A half hour on, they were again in dense brush and Matilda Gage wailed, "I can go no further!"

Instead of ignoring her, usually his way with the women's complaints, McCormick halted, dismounted, and went to her. Holding up his arms, he allowed her to slide down from her saddle and held her for a moment after she landed. "We will rest a while," he said.

"But it is hardly past noon," Margaret protested, glancing at the sun.

"The horses will break down if we keep on at this pace," McCormick told her as he fetched a blanket out of his saddlebag and spread it on the ground. "Sit," he commanded, and the other women slid down from their horses and, obediently, sat. John, released, skipped a little before settling in Margaret's lap. The horses began to pull at the scant grass.

They rested, Margaret figured, for the best part of an hour as the sun inched westward across the sky. McCormick drew out his pipe, loaded it with his foul-smelling tobacco, and began to smoke.

Seeing him seemingly at ease, Margaret asked him, "Which of us do you intend to leave first?"

But she had presumed too far. As Caroline laid a warning hand on her arm, McCormick jerked upright and ordered them to mount. The brief truce was over. "Do not question him again," Caroline whispered as they hurried to their horses. "He is not accustomed to questions from females." Matilda, still protesting, limped along behind them and had to be helped by the other women to mount.

As they moved forward into the brush, Caroline began to sing, "Go tell it on the mountain." It was an old song they all knew, and they joined in the words: "That Jesus Christ is born." Even McCormick added his baritone.

John, who had been sleeping clamped to McCormick's back, woke up and howled. Riding up, Margaret began to sing, "Hush Little Baby, don't you cry," and after a few verses, John dropped off to sleep again.

The song reminded Margaret of her two precious books, lost when the first Shawnee village was burned. Their words stretched back to Virginia, to Pennsylvania, and even to Scotland and England. It was the first connection she'd felt to her past in a long time and it was, briefly, comforting. She wondered if she would ever remember the lines she'd written in the blank spaces in the almanack.

She began to feel the frail tug of the bonds that still bound her to the Greenbrier Settlement. Even when her daily life with the Shawnee had lost some of its absorbing strangeness, even when, after the first year, the tribe's demands on her time and energy had become manageable, or nearly, she had seldom thought of the place she was now trying to call home, or of her mother, brothers and sisters. And she had nearly forgotten her dead husband as her new life rushed her forward.

Now the pang of losing John cut her to the quick. As her horse stumbled through a rocky stream and clambered up a steep bank, she remembered her last glimpse of him, mortally wounded, running, his hand pressed to the blood flowing from his side.

Margaret knew now that in spite of their brief marriage and the birth of their first child, she had hardly known John Paulee. She thought of the way years together would have unfolded his character, how she would have learned him as he aged. The bitterest loss seemed now to be the loss of that future. She had only known him as a very young man, sweet but untested. They had both missed everything that was to come. She reached up to feel the unaccustomed tear beneath her right eye.

And then their murdered daughter. She wept as she had never wept before. The other women rode silently behind her, preserving her from what she did not want or need.

At the next stream, McCormick ordered a halt to water the horses and let John slide down. "You take him now," he told Margaret. John was hopping from foot to foot, and Margaret saw a hint of his old liveliness.

She leaned down from her saddle to hoist him up, and his slight weight in her arms felt for an instant no greater than the weight of her murdered daughter. Settling John in front of her, she tried to imagine how she might have saved her, how she might have fought the savagery of her captors rather than almost at once accepting it as essential to her survival. Could she have found the strength in her arms to hold her daughter? She knew such an outcome was unlikely, but she wished now that she had offered her head in trade to be smashed against the tree. She knew that her sacrifice would not have saved her daughter. But even the attempt, had word crept back to the Greenbrier, would have sweetened her reputation. It was a low thought, but necessary.

As they plodded again through heavy brush, Caroline, who had been watching her, rode up. "Are the demons about, dear?" she asked, leaning toward Margaret, portly and comforting. "Are they scratching at your soul?"

"My husband," Margaret told her. "My daughter. Both dead. And I hardly knew him."

"We must believe they have gone to a better place," Caroline said, and Margaret felt the thinness of her comfort. "Let us sing again, to lift our hearts." She began to thump out, "I walked in the valley alone, when the dew was still on the roses," and continued to the end of three verses, her deep contralto sufficient alone. The others did not know the words. "He walks with me and He talks with me and He tells me I am his own," she repeated the refrain. "He walks with you as well, Margaret."

"Better that he rides with me," she said dryly.

"That He assuredly does." Caroline continued to keep beside Margaret whenever she could until they stopped at sundown.

They had ridden into a small clearing, edged with sycamore and pine. In front of them stood a plain square cabin, protected by a log palisade. The second story of the cabin was pierced with portholes from which, Margaret knew, the people inside could fire at invaders. The stout gates in the palisade were closed, and all was silent and still.

McCormick rode forward, waving his hat and hallooing. At once Margaret saw the glint of a flintlock barrel at a porthole.

Almost at the same moment, the gates swung open and a large white woman rushed out, brandishing a stick.

"Mama!" Lucy wailed.

The big woman advanced on her, dragged her down from her saddle, and began belaboring her with the stick.

"I'll learn you!" she screamed. "You whore! Stealing off after the soldiers!"

Lucy crouched, holding up her hands to protect her head. "Mama—"

"Stop!" Margaret shouted. "In the name of God—" Her horse, startled, began to back away, and she had to use all her strength to rein it in.

Suddenly, McCormick lurched down from his saddle and seized the woman's stick. A short, fierce struggle ended abruptly when he wrenched the stick away and broke it over his knee. The old woman, disarmed, began to weep, fat tears crawling down her dirty cheeks. Lucy was still crouching on the ground, her hands over her head.

McCormick helped her up. "Your daughter, ma'am, returned to you by the grace of God and through my efforts," he said.

"By God I paid not a penny, 'twas her brother who got up the ransom, said it was a shame on the family to leave her with the savages," the old woman protested.

"Nevertheless, the ransom was paid and here is the result," McCormick said.

Lucy was staring at her mother. "Mama," she whispered, but the big woman turned without a word and disappeared inside the gates.

McCormick took down Lucy's saddlebags. He pushed them into her arms. "Go," he ordered, tying her horse to the fence post.

Lucy stood, hesitating, looking at him beseechingly.

"We cannot leave her here," Margaret told him.

"We have no choice. That is my directive, and I was paid for her only this far."

Caroline rode up beside Margaret. "They will make up, in time," she said. But Margaret had seen the look of terror on Lucy's thin face.

McCormick gave the girl a shove, then mounted and turned his horse toward the woods. Margaret found herself following with the other two women riding close behind her. Looking back, she saw Lucy gaping after them as the gates of the palisade closed.

CHAPTER TWENTY

A FTER CAMPING that night in a mountain hollow near a running stream edged with reeds, the starving horses stripped, the four travelers rode up to the crest and paused to survey what lay before them. Folds of mountains, divided by sharp valleys, subsided gradually into hills, and then a stretch of nearly level ground, far to the East.

"There're settlements round about there," McCormick said, pointing with his stick at thin plumes of smoke rising from the valleys. "Settlers' cabins, been here quite a while."

As they rode along the spine of the mountains, Matilda kicked her limping bay to plod up beside McCormick. "I believe my place is in that far valley," she told him.

"Within striking distance," McCormick agreed, spurring ahead.

Matilda fell back beside Margaret. "I'm old," she said. "I was afeared they'd none of them want me back, but then my sister got the money together."

"How much?"

"Two hundred," Matilda said proudly. "My tribe was glad to let me go for that. Lucy was gone even longer. Five years, and still she didn't get a warm welcome."

"Poor girl," Margaret said, remembering the palisade gates closing. "What will become of her now?"

McCormick, waiting for them on the bluff, answered sharply. "Back to her old trade. Militia pass this way often."

Margaret did not reply.

Matilda said gently, "Oh, surely not."

"Apple never falls far from the tree. That old dame made a good living."

They rode down the bluff in silence. Margaret felt Matilda's anticipation like a current of warm air at her back. Matilda wanted to go home. Margaret regretted that she'd never asked Lucy whether she desired to be returned. She had been stopped by her own perplexity, her confused feelings of fear, regret, and a shimmer of hope.

She spoke to Caroline over her shoulder. "Do you wish to go back?"

"Back to the savages?" Caroline asked incredulously.

"Back to your own people."

"Four years I've longed for it, prayed every night for my safe return. They finally gathered the money. Two hundred dollars— they need me, you see. I'm the best weaver in the place. Since I was taken, no new rugs or blankets for cold nights. Yes," she added expansively, "I will be welcomed, I believe. Not like poor Lucy."

"I admire your good fortune," Margaret said.

"May yours be the same."

At the bottom of the next hill, a narrow valley opened out to a cluster of cabins, the largest settlement Margaret had seen. "There it is!" Matilda cried, riding forward and, for the first time, leading the way.

They entered the settlement and clattered down a sort of road, paved with rough stones. At the noise, women appeared in their doorways, staring.

A large two-story cabin stood at the end of the road, a sign swinging and creaking in the wind. Above a crude painting of a whiskey jug, broad lettering in red spelled out, GAGE'S SALOON ALL WAYFARERS WELCOME.

Matilda dropped from her horse and crouched low, hobbling to the door. She pounded on it with both fists until it was opened from the inside and she nearly fell, caught under the arms by a withered stick of a man who yelled, "So ye've come back, Matilda!"

Margaret had not imagined that the gentle widow was in any way connected to a saloon keeper.

McCormick dismounted, unleashed Matilda's saddlebags, carried them to the door, and dropped them at her feet.

"What have we here?" the saloonkeeper asked, kicking the bags. "Ill-gotten gains! You went from here raw, plucked up in naught but your shift."

Matilda bridled. "I was dressed the night of my capture as I am now, Emos. The saddlebags hold two blankets my tribe gave me."

"I'll have naught of their plunder," Emos Gage said, kicking the saddlebags back toward McCormick, who ignored them. Without a word, he went to Matilda's horse and tied it to the hitching post with the reins. The Gages disappeared into the cabin, the door closing sharply behind them. Matilda had not even said goodbye.

McCormick beckoned to Margaret and Caroline. "Emos Gage never would part with a penny to bring her back," he grumbled. "'Twas the neighbors paid the ransom."

"She assured me she was a widow, her husband murdered on the trail," Margaret told him as they rode out of the settlement.

"Few women stay widow long," McCormick said with a laugh.

"No need to wait for the circuit rider when a man's bed is cold."

Behind her, Caroline laughed. Margaret felt foolish and at the same time, an unexpected sadness as the loss of Matilda and even of Lucy swept over her. She knew they would never cross paths again. Remembering the long winter months when they had worked together to clean McCormick's cabin and the stews they had stirred over the cooking fire while Caroline sang her old songs, Margaret turned in her saddle to plead, "I'm down at heart, Caroline. Sing me one of your ditties."

"Hardly ditties," Caroline objected, but then she launched into "Jerusalem, My Happy Home." Margaret wondered whether Caroline was the only one of the four who expected a happy home at the end of their journey. Lucy's welcome had been no welcome and Margaret could not imagine the scene inside the Gage Saloon.

They halted in the next valley to water the horses at a meandering stream and to chew a little hard tack.

"Hark, the little owl," Caroline said as the creature hooted softly from the branch behind them. "She has been following us since morning."

Margaret objected, "It's nearly noon. Owls are not likely to be abroad."

"No matter to her. She's led me home before when I was after a lost cow in this very valley."

McCormick laughed as he filled his canteen at the stream. "She'll lead us into the briary bush," he said, jerking a shoulder at the dense brush on the other side of the stream.

"That she'll never do." Caroline cocked her head toward the owl's soft cry, which had moved a little way off. "Our way is along this stream. Crookshank is its name."

McCormick hung back to allow Caroline to take the lead. Margaret followed, marveling. The little owl went ahead of them, hidden in the brush, and its cry reminded Margaret of how she had learned to discern owl calls from Indians' warning hoots. She nearly spoke of it, then realized it had no meaning now.

They rode along Crookshank Creek until the brush gave way to open pasture, and then Caroline led them up the bank. Margaret was awed by her knowledge, which seemed to show a blood connection to the brush, the creek, and the open field. She did not know the country around the Greenbrier so thoroughly, but her family had possessed no cattle for her to chase. It occurred to her suddenly that knowing the country might mean finding a home in it.

Leading the way across a pasture dotted with browsing cows, Caroline pointed to a stout two-story house, made of frame, not logs, with the glass in many windows winking in the westering sun. Smoke was rising from a heavy chimney of bricks, not river stones, and the front of the house was decorated with a small white-painted porch supported by two slender columns. Blue Jacket's had been the only house of similar size and elegance Margaret had seen.

Caroline kicked her exhausted horse into a trot. "Husband! Ethan!" she shouted at the top of her lungs as the other horses stumbled after her.

The door of the cabin opened and a large old man came out. He wore his mottled gray hair long over his shoulders, but he was clean-shaven, dressed in the black trousers and long coat of a city dweller with the first red cravat Margaret had ever seen.

Caroline dropped from her horse and rushed to him. He caught her, then held her off, examining her face. Two black women, alerted by Caroline's shouting, came to peer over his shoulder.

"A long time gone, Husband!" Caroline gasped.

"We thought ye dead for sure. Well, you've come through it tolerable well, not much loss of flesh," he said, feeling her hips. She giggled, slapping his hand away. Then, without a word to the others, he led Caroline into the house, the two black women turning toward the back door.

A moment later, he returned and went up to McCormick. "I owe you the promised sum," he said, taking a purse out of his pocket.

"I brought her back to you with that understanding," McCormick said, "and no down payment, seeing as you are known around here as a man of your word."

"Softly, softly," the big man said. "I pay on delivery as I told you three months ago."

"The others were ransomed ahead of time, as is the custom. I was paid before I took them. And now I have delivered your wife to you," McCormick said, holding out his hand. "Two hundred dollars, Mister."

The big man hesitated, his purse in his hand. "She has not been damaged?"

"That is beyond my knowledge, but she was much prized by the Cherokee for her weaving skill. It was only on my promise of a large ransom that they were persuaded to release her."

"I will depend on it, then," the big man said, counting Spanish dollars into McCormick's palm. Glancing at Margaret, he went on, "We hear dreadful tales. But then, my wife is old." He turned back toward the house.

"Are we not to say farewell?" Margaret asked.

"If you wish this to be your last night sleeping on the ground, we must press on," McCormick said, turning his horse.

Margaret craned back at the house, hoping to see Caroline at one of the flashing windows, but there was no one.

CHAPTER TWENTY-ONE

BY RIDING HARD through open country as long as they could see their way with the help of the full moon—Margaret estimated they rode until nearly midnight—they reached the brow of a hill overlooking the Greenbrier Settlement. Because of the full moon, the settlement was still astir. Margaret spied her mother's cabin, which stood near the entrance to the town, and a group of people lit by the flames of a cookfire.

As she and McCormick rode closer, Margaret studied each face in the group around the fire, but the only one she recognized at first was her younger sister. Eliza was now a toothpick-thin young woman, barefooted, as they all were, her worn cotton shift drooping from one shoulder. She was engaged in tearing bits of meat off a large leg bone to offer to two smaller children whom Margaret did not recognize. Looking up, Eliza stared at her.

Their mother was nowhere to be seen.

How chill and strange it was, Margaret thought, to be able to name only one member of her family. Four years had changed them completely. She knew she also had changed greatly, her upper arms thickened by the legions of logs she had split and carried, her shoulders broadened after years of carrying spring water, her fair complexion damaged and darkened.

She watched other people gathering on their cabin doorsteps, scanning the strangers with alarm. Arriving at this late hour boded no good. Were they in flight from another burned stockade or raided cabin? A man grabbed a cowbell and began to ring it vigorously and more people tumbled out of their doors, some wearing nightshirts and caps.

As they rode into the settlement, Margaret recognized the big tulip poplar, long spared the ax because of the children's pleading. One branch, a few feet from the ground and twenty feet long, had always provided a sort of swing. Margaret remembered her brothers ranged along the branch, stoutly kicking the dirt to set it swinging. They were sitting and swinging now, released from bed by the excitement.

She began to recognize them in spite of the large and small changes their time apart had wrought. The oldest four were all taller but thin as rakes.

Quickly, she named them.

The eldest boy was now a young man with a whisp of blond beard on his chin, far too old to swing on the poplar branch: Ethan.

The brother next in line was still mostly a child, his face scarred from what must have been a bout with smallpox. He had the long, bruised legs of a forest runner, and Margaret remembered he had always been a wild thing closer to a deer than to a boy: Charlie.

Next was a grinning fourteen-year-old with a mop of red hair, the only one of the brood with that coloring: James, never called Jimmy, by their mother's decree.

The fourth in age was a tall creature who had outgrown his clothes, his pants not reaching his ankles, his wrists hanging below his sleeves, his great bare feet broad as shovels: Winston, who had been her favorite lap child.

Looking back, Margaret saw Eliza beside the fire, still tearing off bits of meat for the two youngest boys. These little ones were chewing rapidly, standing shoulder to shoulder as though aspiring to be joined in the flesh. They were scarcely a year apart and were perhaps three and two years old. They showed the depredations of the hard winter just passed in a shadowy fairness that warned, Margaret thought, that they would not be long for this world.

The smallest of the two was staring at her. Riding close to him, Margaret leaned down and asked his name.

"Abraham," he told her, speaking thickly, and she saw that he had a cleft palette that split his upper lip and turned the edges upward. She remembered hearing that babies born late in a woman's life tended to enter the world with injuries that hardly equipped them to survive.

She leaned down again to ask the other small boy his name. He looked up at her brightly and said, "Peter. On this rock I will build my church."

Margaret was for the first time truly astonished. "Who told you that?" she asked.

"My paw. He's the preacher."

"So now you have a church?"

He turned to point to a little structure at the edge of the settlement with a wide door and a tiny steeple, topped with a white cross.

Margaret said to McCormick, "There was no church here when I was taken."

McCormick nodded grimly. "The Methodists send their missionaries far and wide, making great difficulties for those of us inclined to sip a little rum. These days I spend no time in this settlement."

Now, alerted by the commotion and the cowbell, the family's cabin door opened and the mother of them all stepped out, carrying a sleeping infant on her arm.

She stared at Margaret, who felt her old affection for her mother welling up in tears. How worn her mother looked, how much older than when Margaret had left.

Riding up to her, McCormick told her, "The young Shawnee chief accepted your two hundred dollars, although the squaws did not wish to let your daughter go."

Still she was silent and staring. The rest of the family was also silent and staring.

"Go to your grandma," Margaret told John as McCormick dropped him from his saddle. He stood uncertainly, looking up at his mother. "Go!" she ordered and he trotted away to the woman standing in the cabin doorway.

Occupied with this strange homecoming, Margaret did not notice McCormick turning his horse. "Good luck to you!" he shouted at the edge of the settlement, but when she started to answer, he had already ridden into the trees.

She dismounted and tied her horse to the iron-topped hitching post that stood outside the tavern next door. The hitching post she remembered, but the tavern surprised her; it had been old Tomasita Luckett's cabin, but now it displayed a sign welcoming all comers above the familiar image of an earth-colored whiskey jug.

She went to her mother's cabin. There was no more excuse for delay. As she approached, she saw that John was standing looking up at his grandmother with the fearlessness he had learned among the Shawnee. Nancy was staring at him without expression.

Then she crouched to examine him, and Margaret saw that she

was wearing the old blue-checked homespun gown she remembered, much the worse for wear.

As Margaret watched, Nancy tipped up the little boy's chin with her forefinger. John did not flinch, although he raised his hand to remove her finger.

Nancy stood up. "I see nothing of John Paulee in him," she told Margaret.

Margaret said hurriedly, "Surely you see his father's eyes, bright blue, with black lashes and eyebrows—put in with a sooty finger, you used to say."

"Half the men hereabouts have those Irish eyes," Nancy said, shifting the infant to the other arm, "and the little savages too, I've heard tell, because of their barbarous ways with our women captives."

"I saw no signs of such behavior!"

"Enough," Nancy said. "Come inside." She beckoned to the other children, who were watching open-mouthed. "In, all of you."

As they herded inside, Margaret's brother Ethan touched her shoulder. "She used to cry for you every night."

Margaret nodded. She would need to give her mother time. But it was bitter to meet with this reception. "Has Mother married again while I was away?" she asked him.

"Three years ago come Michaelmas. He's the preacher here now, Mr. Rutherford Thompson, sent to us from the mission. Gone most of the time to see to his other parishes but here once a month on God's day to preach his sermon."

"Then these two—?" Margaret asked, pointing to the two little boys who had followed their mother to the stove.

"His. That last one, too. Born three months ago and baptized

Christian-like. Mr. Thompson says we must all go through it, but I claim I'm too old to duck my head for a splash of water, holy or not."

"Perhaps when Mr. Thompson arrived, Mother stopped crying for me," Margaret said dryly. Her brother did not answer.

Now Nancy ordered him to fetch a bucket of water from the spring, which ended their talk.

Her mother still had not greeted her, although Margaret felt the weight of her eyes. Now she beckoned her into the cabin, then set her to chopping winter-dug potatoes, hard as brown stones, to add to the deer meat stew that was steaming in an iron pot over the fire. The potatoes were hardly cooked before the children came, each with a spoon, to dip and try the supper, then snatched tin plates and lined up as Nancy doled out portions. As each child passed, Margaret noticed, Nancy examined it, parting hair to check for lice, pinching a dirty cheek. Likely it was the first time she'd seen them since sunup.

Nancy had still to greet Margaret. She handed her a tin plate grudgingly as though there was not enough for another mouth, and indeed she'd had to scrape the bottom of the iron pot.

Dinner was soon eaten. When the plates had been taken to the spring and washed, each child responsible for his own, Nancy shooed them all up to the loft. Eliza had gone out.

John had chosen to sit during supper with red-haired James, and they had scuffled and laughed together. Now he went up to the loft with the others. The romping and yelling continued for a time until Nancy shouted for silence.

"Devils," she said amiably, settling herself in the one chair with arms. "But better than girls with their ways." She took up a nearly finished sock and began to knit.

"Does Eliza have troublesome ways?" Margaret asked with an innocence she almost felt.

"Not to your measure. You remember how you used to do, out at all hours, up to no good. A fine thing it was John Paulee married you when he did or I'd have had a bastard on my hands."

Margaret was silent. There was too much time and space between them and no quick way to bridge it.

Nancy laid down the sock and gestured to Margaret to hold out her hands so the new skein of yarn, dun-colored like the rest, could be stretched between them. She began to wind off the yarn rapidly. "Now ye've brought me a wood's colt," she grumbled.

Again Margaret said nothing. After a moment, she asked, "How are you, Mother?"

"Worn down with work, dawn to dusk," Nancy replied promptly. She placed her hand over the small swell in her apron. "And another this summer."

"Your new husband—?"

"Gone three weeks out of four, riding his circuit. A good man, a servant of the Lord," she added, a phrase Margaret had never heard on her mother's lips. "Comes home randy as a billy goat, telling me my duty." She glanced at the baby in the worn cradle by the fire. "That one there come close to killing me."

Margaret did not choose to go in that direction. "Where is Eliza?" she asked.

"Running wild, same as you. She'll be back here late without a doubt."

Again Margaret chose not to go further. "I remember her a little girl," she said.

"Four years is a long time, Margaret."

John came creeping down the loft ladder, looking for his mother, but Nancy shooed him up again. "If he's to stay here with us awhile, he must learn our ways," she said. "Acts like a little savage, so bold."

"He is John Paulee's son."

"How can that be, Daughter? You lit out of here with a suckling babe and even I never conceived while I was nursing."

"Nevertheless—" Margaret felt her face growing hot.

"Well, you'll be going back to the savages soon, and the boy, too," Nancy said, taking the skein of yarn and beginning to wind it into a ball. "Never heard of a redeemed captive that wanted to stay with her kind."

Margaret looked at her mother, bent over her yarn. The broad planes of her cheeks and forehead gleamed in the firelight, carved with wrinkles. This was not the same woman who had run after her on leaving day, shouting, "Teach, Daughter! Teach!"

Four years, endless toil, three more children. Margaret shuddered. There seemed little hope of a bridge between them.

She went to look at the infant in her cradle by the fire. The little girl seemed to be sleeping deeply, but her cheeks were flushed with fever. "When will you give her suck?" she asked her mother.

Nancy did not look up from her yarn. "She is poorly. The tit does not interest her."

"Perhaps a sugar titty, then?"

Nancy shook her head. "She'll cry when she's hungry. A waste of time else."

Margaret laid her palm on the infant's hot cheek. "She is running fever. Is there no one to help?"

"Old man Peters claimed to know the herbs better than me.

Dead and laid to rest these six months and my man forbids me the practice, says it's not the way of Christians. Spring is always the time for fevers. She'll pull out of it by morning, Lord willing."

As Margaret stood watching, the tiny body was shaken by a violent spasm. She moaned and curled. Margaret remembered the old chief on his deathbed, showing her a point in the sky. But this infant had no sky to call her own.

CHAPTER TWENTY-TWO

T HE INFANT DIED during the night without a whimper, as
though unwilling to disturb her sleeping family. Margaret,
who had spent the night in the loft to be with John, found her
shortly after dawn. Her mouth was ringed with blood, her eyes
were open and fixed. Her body was locked in a spasm.

She called for her mother and together they worked over the
dead baby to loosen and straighten her limbs. Sliding down the
ladder from the attic, the other children came one by one to look.
John stood staring in silence and did not follow the other children
when they ran outdoors.

Nancy stopped Charlie and told him to go for Tom the joiner, to
measure the infant for her coffin. An hour later, Margaret heard the
snarl of his saw, shortening the pine boards. By midday the box was
ready, and Nancy lined it with leaves before laying the tiny girl inside.
As Tom nailed down the lid, Nancy looked at Margaret. "My change
of life child," she said, "and promised to be no trouble in this world."

"Or in the next," Margaret said to fill the gap.

Nancy looked at her sharply. "Did the missionaries visit your
savages?"

"No, but this is the Indian way. All is pattern and repetition.
As in this world, so in the next. Perhaps your missionaries believe
the same."

"They believe in saving our souls," Nancy said quickly.

"I never heard you talk of souls before," Margaret ventured.

Nancy flushed with anger. "Your sister is nailed in her coffin! Do you think I could endure her death and all the others—the settlement lost two half-grown children and three babies this past winter—without a shred of hope for the hereafter?"

Margaret asked quietly, "Then you have come to believe in heaven?"

"I must!" Nancy's voice rose to fill the cabin. Then, lowering her voice, she ordered, "Enough of this idle chatter. Help me prepare the hominy. It calls for washing in three waters and overnight soaking."

"I know." Margaret stood up and fetched the bucket. "I do not recollect you preparing hominy before."

"The traders visit us more now. We have a greater choice of provisions."

As Margaret took the path to the spring, she saw that someone had planted a handful of bulbs along the way, jonquils, springing up green-leafed and peaked with tightly folded buds. Had the traders brought such a luxury, who in the hard-pressed settlement would have had the money to buy or the time to plant them?

Kneeling down, she pressed one slender, tight bud to her cheek. It was cold. If such things were to be found, she vowed to buy and plant jonquil bulbs where her infant died, then knew she would never be able to find that tree in the forest.

After washing the hominy in cold spring water, rinsing it, then washing it again, Margaret carried the hominy back to the cabin and submerged it in a pot of boiling water. The children were clamoring at the door, but she did not let them in. Old ways came back to her before she expected them. Even John was closed out with the rest.

She skinned the rabbit she found in the cold larder, gutted it, and threw the entrails out the window for the dogs. Then she split the rabbit into parts with the cleaver, tossed the parts in corn meal, and dropped them into boiling bear fat spitting on the stove. The smell of the meat, rich and gamey, brought moisture to Margaret's mouth, and the children at the door knocked harder. When at last Nancy lifted the latch, they rushed in, beginning at once to grumble over the small portions their mother dished onto their tin plates. John ate as greedily as the rest. Afterward they all rushed outside and John, a little dolefully, followed them.

Toward sunset, as Margaret was building up the fire and Nancy was tending to her mending, a tall man came into the cabin without knocking. Alarmed, Margaret turned to face him, then saw to her surprise that her mother had emptied her lapful of torn garments onto the floor and was rushing toward the stranger. He stretched out a long arm and hooked her to his side, and Margaret saw something she had never seen before: her mother burying her face in the stranger's shoulder.

He patted her twice, looking over her head at Margaret. "Come," he said, "make me known to your staring daughter."

Nancy lifted her face and turned to Margaret. "Daughter, this is my husband," she said.

"I presume you are Margaret," the tall man said. "I heard talk of your coming back when I held a burial service yesterday the next town over. Chattering women pass news quickly around here." He spoke meticulously, advancing toward her and holding out his broad, long-fingered hand. "I am Preacher Thompson, your mother's husband these three years," he said.

Margaret felt him press her fingers warmly. He was looking her over with a faint smile. "None the worse for wear, I see," he said. "Saved by the grace of God. We will talk of your baptism when the time is right."

"You'll want to see your sons," Nancy said, but before she could call them, Preacher Thompson held up his hand. "Allow me a little time to become acquainted with this young person."

Nancy vacated her chair by the fire and retreated to a bench in the corner with her mending. Thompson settled himself in the chair, stretching his long legs to the fire. "A weary hard ride," he explained, sighing. "Rain the other side of the mountain and no shelter at all. All the way from Spring Grove in that cold rain. Ethan was prompt to take my horse, I believe the little lecture I gave him last week about the duties of a son has borne fruit."

"Stepson," Margaret corrected, remembering how fond their father had been of his first boy.

"We keep no such distinctions here," the preacher said. "All are equal in my eyes, as they are equal in the eyes of God."

Margaret thought of her sister Eliza and wondered if she would ever see her again.

She went to the door and found John loitering there. Bringing him inside, she told the preacher, "Then you will be pleased to welcome my son." He went to the preacher promptly, looking up into his face without fear. "Are you my father now?" he asked in Shawnee.

The preacher regarded him silently. "Your mother had news of this," he said. "It caused her great grief."

"How is that, Mother?" Margaret turned to Nancy in her corner.

"I prayed that you would come home without such evidence of ill-treatment," Nancy replied, "or, even worse, of a willingness to enter into a heathen alliance."

"John is my husband John Paulee's son, born eight months after my captivity." The words went dry in Margaret's mouth.

Nancy sighed. "Please God that it be so."

"It *is* so!" Margaret raised he voice, exasperated. John crept to her side and clung to her.

The minister intervened. "We heard from a trader that the Shawnee did not wish to let the boy go," he said evenly. "They seemed to believe he was one of them by birth."

"They had grown fond of him," Margaret said, controlling her impatience. "And because of the number of deaths we have inflicted on then, they are eager for replacements. I was adopted to take the place of Chief White Bark's dead daughter."

"In that event," the minister said, stretching his legs, "why did you not choose to stay?"

"It was not my choice," Margaret said, betrayed by her impatience into a confession that would cost her dear. "It was the ransom money. The young chief could not bring himself to refuse it. That sum means relief from hardship for the tribe, at least briefly."

"I see," the minister said with the same imperturbable calm. "It seems you accepted your situation. In that case it becomes even more urgent that I baptize you both—you, your son, and our infant."

John was grasping her skirt with both hands. "What is that man going to do to me?" he whispered in Shawnee.

Margaret laid her hand on his head. "You have nothing to fear," she said in the same language.

"Does he not speak the Christian tongue?" the preacher asked, but before Margaret could answer, her mother said, "All in good time, Rutherford, all in good time. Now I must tell you that our infant girl died during the night and is already in her coffin."

A shadow passed over the preacher's face. "How is that? She was in fine fettle when I left here three weeks ago."

"I do not know, Husband. Some fever or ague, perhaps. She died so quietly I did not know she was passing. I did not have a chance to dose her with my herbs."

"Which would not have saved her," the preacher said. "We must begin to use new ways. I spoke to a physician in Fredericksburg who is considering removing here. We would not have lost her if she had had his ministrations."

Nancy was silent, bending over her work.

"Well," Preacher Thompson said, recovering his composure. "The Lord gives and the Lord taketh away. Blessed is the name of the Lord."

Now the other children rushed in. Thompson beckoned to the two youngest boys, who came and perched on his knees. John watched as the big man embraced them with both arms.

"Is my dinner ready?" the preacher asked. Nancy stood up at once and went to the stove. She served the preacher first with a fine rabbit thigh and a heap of hominy. The children were still watching. Margaret dished out what was left onto their tin plates.

The preacher gnawed the last shred of meat off the rabbit thigh, then stood to command attention. Opening his throat to a voice that filled the cabin as the roar of a winter wind filled the stone chimney, he prayed, "We bless you, Holy Father, for the food you have given us, miserable sinners. Let us all beware of the sin of gluttony when we are presented with such a feast. Let us always remember the fasting your sacred Son undertook to purify himself before his crucifixion. Amen."

The children and Nancy joined in the amen. Only Margaret sat in silence.

"Will you not join us in the blessing?" the preacher asked.

"She does not know the words," Nancy explained quickly. "She will learn soon enough."

The children filed out to scrub their plates with leaves, then plunge them in the washing kettle water. Margaret heard the shouting and jibbing among them that she remembered. John stayed at her side.

The preacher went to the door and summoned them back. Then, as they knelt in front of him, he commenced another prayer. It ended with a blessing for "The Father, the Son, and the Holy Ghost." Quietly, Margaret translated the words into Shawnee for John.

John knew about ghosts from the tales the Shawnee told around their fires. He looked at his mother with alarm. "Is the ghost coming here?" he asked in Shawnee.

"Only if you are naughty," the preacher interposed, and Margaret realized with surprise that he knew their language. She found a grain of hope in that, but John was not comforted.

After the prayer, Nancy ordered the children up to the loft. Margaret followed, unwilling to leave John alone with his fears. Looking back from the ladder, she again saw her mother resting her forehead against the preacher's shoulder while he held her close with one arm.

What did it mean, she wondered, other than a new infant every year. And the next one, Nancy's tenth, might be the one that would bring her to her grave.

Margaret was still awake in the loft when Eliza came creeping in. She beckoned her sister and held her in whispered conversation. The girl was well-grown with red-gold hair that reminded Margaret of Agatha, but her hair was uncombed, falling over her pert unsmiling face.

"Where have you been at this late hour, Eliza?" she whispered.

"Not running away with the savages. I leave that to you," the girl said.

"One day I will tell you the truth of that," Margaret said, holding out the coverlet so the girl could climb in. They huddled together for warmth; the kitchen fire had long since gone out.

Next morning, they buried the infant girl, who had never been named. Margaret and the preacher dug the hole on a hillside near the settlement where a few wooden crosses tilted. It would have been expected to ask neighbor men to dig the hole, but Margaret and her stepfather agreed that the job was best done by the baby girl's kin. It was long and hard labor to dig the six-foot-deep grave in the rocky soil, and as they labored together, Margaret saw shadows cross the preacher's face she would never have expected, shadows of sadness and despair.

When it was done, they carried the little wooden coffin to the edge and Nancy threw a handful of daffodil buds onto it. Then they labored to lower it gently with the aid of two ropes Ethan had brought. When the little box was settled at the bottom, they all began to shovel and throw in the dirt until the hole was finally filled. The preacher tamped the dirt down with his boots. He prayed, "Dear Lord, take thou this little soul," then stopped, his voice clotted with tears.

They turned away in silence. Later, Margaret thought, there would be a marker, another frail wooden cross, tipping toward the earth after a few winters.

CHAPTER TWENTY-THREE

ALL SUMMER MARGARET labored to fulfill her duty to her family and especially to her mother, still exhausted from her pregnancy and the difficult birth of her tenth child, the little girl named Rachel. Margaret guessed that the preacher had chosen the little girl's name; he had made mention of a passage from his scriptures that seemed to Margaret to mean this girl, if she lived, would follow after her mother, or something of that sort. Defying tradition, Thompson had chosen the name as soon as the child was born and her baptism a week later seemed to Margaret to weld her to the earth, and indeed Rachel did live and flourish.

Nancy's only brief respite from nursing the wailing child came when Margaret took Rachel on her lap, offering her a sugar titty. When she saw her mother sink back into the chair and close her eyes, Margaret felt a satisfaction sweet as a spoon of honey, although often it was followed by a sip of the gall of guilt. Her mother had endured three births without help during Margaret's absence.

She understood then as she had never understood or even imagined before what her absence had cost her mother. This was not at first mentioned between them, but as cold weather closed in, it seemed to Margaret that her mother's coolness toward John— she never touched him or took him in her arms—might be laid down to what his existence had cost Nancy.

Finally, Nancy raised the question while they were shelling walnuts for the Christmas cake. "We heard Agatha got taken to Detroit and married a fine gentleman there," she said. "Two winters ago they passed by here for a visit and she was wearing a red velvet cloak. By then," she added somberly, "her mother here had died of her eighth, and what was left of that family went on back East."

"I saw my sister once after her ransom," Margaret allowed. "She has a face to win her a fortune."

"You are not uncomely yourself," Nancy said.

"Chief White Bark perhaps thought so; he would never have let me go." She added quickly, "I was his adopted daughter. I was safe as long as he lived, but his son would have felt no such obligation to keep me. And then he was killed in one of our battles and it was the custom for everything of his to be sacrificed."

Nancy sniffed. "Our battles?"

"We are usually the cause as we try to drive them out of their land."

"How did you escape?"

"Traded for a white man's rifle."

"We know from Scripture that we belong to our husbands but to be traded for a rifle..."

"I was very grateful," Margaret said. "It allowed me to return to you."

"Which, I think, was not your wish."

Margaret was silent. She felt that her mother had long been disturbed by the suspicions that ran through the settlement like fire through a field of dead grass. John's adherence to the Shawnee language and Shawnee ways signified more now than the color of his eyes. No longer sunbaked, he was as white as Margaret, but he could not be rid of the staunch fearlessness he'd learned with the Shawnee and which people at the Greenbrier called impertinence.

One evening when Margaret came down from the loft, where she had finally succeeded in getting all the children bedded down, Nancy looked up from the thread she was spinning to ask, "Where are the books?" The wheel continued to whir as Margaret explained that they had burned in the first village fire.

It had been so long since she had thought of the books or of the few lines she had written in the blank spaces that she hardly believed in them. They seemed a part of a dream that had been replaced as soon as she reached the first Shawnee camp. Remembering how hard she had worked, she thought at first that work had replaced her reading, but that was not it.

Another evening, still at her wheel, her mother commented, "Jennie Wiley made her escape after less than a year, and she'd been left bound hand and foot in a rock house."

"So I've heard tell," Margaret said, sitting down with a lapful of mending.

"Bound tight with buffalo thongs," Nancy went on, her foot on the pedal keeping the wheel turning. "They say when the savages left a-hunting, she rolled herself into a puddle of rain and lay there till her thongs soaked and loosened, then slipped out and made her way back to her people through the wilderness."

"You are forgetting one thing, Mother," Margaret said dryly.

"And what is that, pray tell?" The wheel halted as Nancy stared at her daughter.

"According to the way they tell it, Jennie Wiley had a dream."

"Ah, the fair-haired man," Nancy said as she started the wheel again.

"He led her with a strange light, they say, through the forest to a mountaintop from whence he pointed out a settlement."

"There were no settlements in that place," Nancy objected.

"I know that, Mother, but perhaps the dream gave her hope of finding one."

John came slithering down the ladder from the loft and went to crouch by the fire until Nancy shooed him up again.

"You had no hope?" she asked, and when Margaret hesitated, her mother laughed. "Daughter, you are not the first and will not be the last to fall prey to the savages' magic. Or," she went on, "am I to believe you had little appetite to return?"

Caught by her mother's suspicions, Margaret distained to struggle. She kept her silence. Time would mend, or time would not. Her mother's affection for her had always been clear and perhaps affection would eventually prevail. In the meantime, she comforted John as well as she could for the coldness with which he was treated.

A week later on the night of the full moon, a neighbor, Mr. Erskine, came by the cabin and asked if he could visit for a while. Nancy asked him to come in, but he preferred to sit on a bench outside the door where he proposed to smoke his pipe. "The foul odor of this Kentucky tobacco would distress your family," he said, exhibiting what in Margaret's experience was a rare care for their comfort. He looked to be a nice, small, round man, without distinction but also without much appetite for unkindness.

After that first visit, Mr. Erskine came by the cabin every few evenings, bringing a brace of rabbits or a basket of hulled corn, then taking up his position with his pipe outside the door. At that hour, Margaret was always occupied with herding the children up to bed and attempting to comfort John, who asked her again and again in Shawnee why they had to remain. Before the last frost, her mother insisted on taking over that duty, telling Margaret with no uncertain words that she should go out and sit on the bench with Mr. Erskine.

He was, she discovered, a pleasant enough bachelor of thirty-two whose ancient mother had been his sole charge until her recent death. He did not scruple to list his holdings: a stout cabin, two hectares of ploughed and planted land, a wagon and team as well as the necessary tools, and four heifers fattening for the autumn slaughter. His cooking pots, he told Margaret, were copper, and he was entirely unencumbered by debt or family. The elder Mr. Erskine, his father, had been a trapper of some renown, and, as the only son, Michael, had kept careful stewardship of a small fortune.

Margaret had not thought of marrying for a second time—or for a third, as the settlement would doubtless whisper. But she had her mother's interests at heart. Her future must be provided for. It seemed unlikely that the preacher would ever give her more than a pittance from his meager pay.

So she listened patiently to Mr. Erskine's account. She was not surprised when the children took to dancing around her, shouting, "Mr. Erskine has come for ye again, Margaret! He has the fire of courtship in his eye!"

Margaret saw no fire, but he seemed a decent man, and she readily understood that he was her only hope of sparing her mother a nearly destitute old age. She noted, too, that Mr. Erskine did not seem opposed to John; in fact, once he offered him a sugar lump.

When he asked her one early spring evening to marry him—stubbing out his pipe beforehand—she gave her consent, without much joy, but also without apprehension.

The next Sunday when her stepfather came to town, they were married, and Margaret carried her few possessions and John to Mr. Erskine's fine new cabin, called Walnut Grove, three miles from the settlement. He had agreed without protest that she could continue to help her mother and had provided stable room for Jenny to carry her back to the Greenbrier every day.

This proved to be a brief time, however, before her third child and Mr. Erskine's first was born. It was a girl, and Margaret noticed with dismay that even as an infant she crowded John out entirely, creating in her father a foolish tenderness Margaret had never seen. She was duly baptized and named Jane.

By then John was six years old and as settled as he would ever be in that place. He had even mastered a few words of English, although he could not seem to learn the necessary forms of polite-ness. But he refused to call Michael Erskine father, and he still asked Margaret from time to time when they were going "home." She did not have the heart to tell him that they were never going back and that the Ohio country could not be home.

Her fears for her son were soon drowned by the births of three more children, all boys, in quick succession. Michael Erskine refused to be controlled and so, as Nancy said, "One at the breast, one in the belly, and one in the cradle." Margaret began to be very weary, and, after her third Erskine child, she was confined by the midwife to her bed until her persistent bleeding was finally staunched.

In spite of the increasing scope of her cares, Margaret found herself becoming interested in the building of her stepfather's new church.

The money was solicited, if not always gathered, less than a year after Margaret's return, but it was another year before the building was commenced with many delays. It was to be built at the Sinks of the Greenbrier, a mile and a half from the settlement.

Perhaps, Margaret reasoned as she rode one soft spring day to the site, her interest in the church would make up for her slight involvement in Walnut Grove. Michael Erskine had begun and finished the house seven months before their marriage and had led her there, a new bride, with John tagging along behind. Although it had been her home for three years, she never felt attached as she had to the lodge in the Shawnee camp.

She found an excuse for the grand name, Walnut Grove, in the fine stand of walnut trees where the cabin perched, on a hill leading down to a stream and a spring house. But the house, really a cabin, in spite of its title was in no way different from or superior to Nancy's; the four rooms were very small. Margaret thought it far too tall because of the second story her husband had added for their swiftly growing family. Having completed that second story, he then turned to building the new church with a group of neighbors, on land fortuitously donated.

Mr. Thompson had benefited from his friendship with one Edward Kenan, who, although a Roman Catholic, was possessed of the spirit of generosity. Mr. Kenan had given the plot of land on which the new church was going up, promising that the plot would be owned by the congregation "as long as the grass shall grow and the streams shall flow." He only asked that the church be called Rehoboth.

Margaret searched out the meaning of the name in the Erskine family Bible, which kept pride of place in the ground floor room her husband had instructed her to call the parlor. She found it in Genesis chapter 26, and laughed when she learned that Rehoboth meant "broad place." The land that Mr. Kenan had given was at the bottom of a steep-sided valley. Her laughter failed when she read that the word also meant a place where the Lord expected the inhabitants to be fruitful. She knew what that meant.

Still, she pored over the plans. Seeing her at this occupation, her husband solicited her opinion: "Give me your thoughts, Margaret. Will it do?" It was a strange pleasure to be consulted in any matter, although sometimes her answers provoked a smile.

She found it easy to agree with him that the women in the congregation should be seated in a broad balcony, built along the three interior walls of the church. There, they would be at eye level with Mr. Thompson when he preached from a pulpit built to the height of the balcony. He would need to climb to the pulpit by means of a ladder, and Margaret suggested that a panel might be constructed in front of the pulpit to shield from view the perhaps ungainly spectacle of the preacher scrambling.

Her husband readily agreed.

According to the plan, the men of the congregation would be seated below the women in the main body of the church, where the words of the preacher's homily might fall on them as heavily as hail. This was Margaret's thought, not her husband's. Having learned something of the habits of the men of the settlement, she felt a good deal of hail would be needed to convert them to holiness. The tavern was too well frequented, and carousing there sometimes went on till all hours. The ways she remembered from her childhood of abstinence and hard work seem to be wearing away, even as their first church moved toward completion. She found the contradiction interesting.

For the parishioners' comfort, Margaret suggested the addition of a large iron stove, but this was not to be.

"The smoke from the chimney would surely alert the savages," Mr. Thompson told her. "They would bar the doors and set fire to the church, destroying us all."

Margaret did not argue with his opinion, merely mentioning that she had not witnessed any such savagery on the part of the Shawnee. As she said the words, she saw a shadow of suspicion cross his face. He, too, perhaps believed that she had become too familiar with her captors.

"In any event," she added hastily, "the presence of horses and wagons tied up outside—"

"That may be," he interrupted her, "but we will have no stove." She suspected that he wanted the hardship of winter cold, endured during his lengthy sermons, as a form of sacrifice and purification.

The entire settlement turned out to raise the roof of the church; the men bringing their tools and the women a plentiful lunch they spread on blankets under the trees. At night, they camped in their wagons or slept on the ground. For three days, the clearing at the bottom of the steep-sided valley was filled with the rasp of saws and the regular pounding of nails. Then Margaret knew what she had missed most since her return, and what had bound her to the Shawnee: this regular gathering to work together.

One morning Margaret brought John, hoping to find a welcome for him, but he ran off into the woods. For an hour she found herself without any of her children, having left the babies with the slave woman, Milly, at Walnut Grove.

Her husband never explained the presence of this slender, silent, light-complected woman, who seemed to have come with the house. At first, Margaret had been discomfited; her family had never owned a slave. She remembered there had been a few in the Greenbrier in the old days, but her family had never had the means to acquire one.

But soon she became accustomed to Milly, who was as quiet as she was helpful. Grateful for another pair of hands, Margaret kept down her discomfort with the woman's bondage. It was a fact of life she had never experienced or considered, but because Milly was so useful to her, she came to feel that her enslavement was too convenient to be questioned.

At the church raising as it was growing hot, John came running. Before Margaret could stop him, he commenced to pull off the breeches she had forced him into that morning and stood forth naked except for his shirt and breechcloth. Margaret heard a startled intake of breath all around her and then her husband dropped his hammer, seized John, and tried to force him back into his breeches.

She stepped forward, whether to stop or aid she did not know. John was still struggling.

"He must learn to dress as all boys do here," Michael gasped. John was giving battle with all his strength.

"The breeches chafe his legs when he runs," Margaret offered.

"Then he must learn to run less," Michael said.

John confronted his stepfather, fists clenched. "I will not!" he shouted.

The women watching tittered, astonished at such a display of impudence.

"And," Michael went on in a lower voice, "you must put him into drawers."

"That will hardly be possible," Margaret objected, staring at her husband's clenched jaw. "I was only able to get him into the breeches by allowing him to wear his breechcloth underneath."

"It is indecent. You must govern him, Wife, rather than permitting him to govern you."

From that moment on, Margaret lost all interest in the new church. She felt quite certain that neither she nor John would ever sit in the congregation.

That night, as she was putting John to bed with the other children in the second-floor room her husband had ordained for them (he allowed her latest infant to sleep in the cradle near their own bed), John began to weep, clinging to her gown and pleading passionately, in Shawnee, "Take me home, Mama. Take me home." She had believed that he had given up this notion, but his battle with his stepfather had renewed his old longing.

"This is our home," Margaret reproved him, but he struck her roundly with his small fists. The tumult brought Michael Erskine up the stairs.

"Wife, you must keep better order," he reproved her, and Margaret, on her knees with John in her arms, did not know how to reply.

In 1791 as soon as the church was finished, an esteemed minister, the Reverend William Phoebus, arrived on horseback from Brooklyn, a seven-day journey. He came to consecrate Rehoboth with bell, book, and candle and to baptize the year's crop of infants as well as the older children newly come to the settlement. John was included in this group, as though by sleight of hand; Margaret realized later that her stepfather had brought it about.

After the first day of instruction, which John had attended most unwillingly, persuaded only by his mother's promise that he would be free the following day to go to the woods, Mr. Thompson came to her, his face solemn with concern. "Your son refuses to kneel," he told her.

Margaret thought to explain that the Shawnee never knelt; only captives marked out for execution were forced to their knees. She realized soon enough that this explanation was no excuse. "I will speak to him," she said.

"Do so at once. He cannot be baptized and receive communion if he will not kneel, which will only further inflame suspicions about him. If he is to live among us, he must be a Christian."

"I will of course do my best. But Christianity is a frail protection. You surely know how the Long Knives murdered the praying Indians, on their knees in the Moravian village."

"An evil rumor," Rutherford Thompson said.

Margaret did not argue, going to find John tucked into a corner of the loft, where he often went now to conceal himself.

"You must learn to kneel," she told him abruptly, then saw that he chose not to understand, and translated the words into Shawnee.

He shook his head with the fierceness she had come, in spite of herself, to respect.

"He will not kneel," she told her stepfather when she found him outside his cabin, chopping wood.

"Then I must bring him to it," the big man said, dropping his ax and drawing off his leather belt.

"No!" Margaret cried, spreading her arms to bar him. She realized later that it was the first time she had defied him. She knew how he would employ his belt, raising it high over his head, the metal buckle shining, before bringing it down on his quivering prey. She had heard his own children screaming when he beat them.

He stared at her with disbelief. "Surely you are not defying me."

Michael Erskine came down the path from the outhouse, stopping short when he saw his wife and his father-in-law.

"He intends to beat John," Margaret said breathlessly.

"With respect." Michael laid his hand on the older man's shoulder. "Should anyone in my household deserve punishment, I will deliver the blows."

The two men glared at each other. Margaret explained hastily, "John is trying with all his might to do what is expected of him here, but sometimes it is too hard."

Slowly, her stepfather was buckling back on his belt. "If he will not kneel, he cannot be baptized and accepted as a member of our congregation."

"There may be worse outcomes," Michael Erskine said, smiling slightly.

"I very much doubt it."

"Faith coerced is not faith, but fear," Michael said, adding, "Perhaps when John is older and has become more accustomed to our ways here."

"Well, he is your son, I suppose," Preacher Thompson said, with a wicked gleam. "I wash my hands of it."

From that moment on, Margaret's stepfather neither looked at nor spoke to John, and the boy was not baptized. Nancy, already suspicious, caught this further contagion and passed it along to her neighbors, and by midwinter John had no playmates other than slave Milly's boy.

And so it went on, month after month, time moving either

swiftly or slowly according to Margaret's disposition. She bore her fifth child to Michael Erskine, a boy she named after his father and whom she knew from the state of her body would be her last. Her husband accepted her decision, wordlessly but without rancor, and moved to another bed.

"You will be worn to a shred," her mother warned her when they were at the wash pot, scrubbing out soiled infant rags. "Pray do not follow my road!" She had given birth to her eleventh in the late fall and was slow at regaining her strength. "Bid your husband contain himself!" Margaret did not tell her that the containment had already begun, leading to a certain coolness between husband and wife.

CHAPTER TWENTY-FOUR

THEN TIME BEGAN to move more slowly, even to drag, as the Erksine children grew up and John reached early manhood.

A moment of speed occurred in the summer of 1809 when Margaret's sister Eliza, the rambunctious redhead much scrutinized by the settlement because of her outlandish ways, was picked up by a roving band of Shawnee when she was out berry picking.

Alarm spread quickly. Several families departed post haste for the nearest fort, and others barricaded themselves in their cabins, dreading depredations. Michael Erskine would not go to the fort, nor did Margaret wish it. He proposed getting together a party posthaste to go after the girl before the savages were away across the Ohio.

"Go with them," Nancy begged Margaret. "You know their language. You know the whereabouts of their camps. Go and plead for your sister."

"If I go, Mother, I will take John and we will never come back." The decision formed in the instant, as she was speaking.

Nancy searched her face. "For shame! And leave everything here on my hands!"

Before Margaret could answer, her mother turned away, casting her words bitterly over her shoulder. "Very well then. I have long perceived that you have little love for your family here. Perhaps you will reunite with the savage we all know is John's father."

Margaret did not reply. She had been expecting her mother's words for a long time. The silences that came between them when they were stripping venison for jerky or nursing a dying fire had a meaning that did not need to be explained. Nancy had never accepted John as a grandson and she had never fully embraced Margaret as her daughter. It was the price Margaret paid, she believed, for all she had learned from the Shawnee.

The search party returned empty-handed. The Shawnee had escaped over the Ohio into their own lands where no white man dared to go.

⚜

As the long, difficult journey back receded from her memory, Margaret noticed that the years began to move rapidly until she was calling the Greenbrier Settlement home. She had never expected to be able to claim it, but once she had, time took on an additional swiftness perhaps, she thought, because her adventures were over. The everyday life of the colony was grueling but monotonous, and there was little to mark the passage from year to the next, except for John's rapid growth.

The coolness between Margaret and her mother lasted and spread rapidly to the rest of the settlers. It was Nancy who voiced the notion that John, now a well-grown lad of nearly twenty, should go and live with Michael Erskine's older brother in Lewisburg. Andrew Erskine was a lawyer, well placed and successful, willing to accept John as an apprentice.

Margaret went looking for her son and found him unslinging his flintlock; he had been hunting wild turkey and brought her three fat hens.

"You have endured much here, my son," she said after thanking him for the birds. "It may be the time has come for you to go to a friendlier place. Your Uncle Andrew has no sons, only a passel of daughters, and he lives in a fine house in Lewisburg. You will attend the academy there and later be trained by your uncle to follow in his footsteps as a lawyer."

John looked at her, his face full of doubt. "We have never yet been separated," he said.

Margaret touched his shoulder. "Lewisburg is but a day's ride from here."

After a moment, John said quietly, "If you wish it," and Margaret remembered how the Shawnees had taught their children always to abide by their elders' wisdom.

"I wish it," she said, knowing it was the only way she could persuade him to leave her. Then she went to assemble his few things.

John rode away before dawn the following day.

After his departure, time galloped.

Now and then, Margaret's mother urged her to gather another ransom for her sister Eliza, gone now for nearly seven years, but Margaret begged her mother to desist. "The Shawnee will have adopted her long since," she explained. "Pray do not try to wrench her away."

"Ah, the barbarians," Nancy cried. "When will we have done with them?"

"I believe they are mostly gone now from our side of the mountains," Margaret said. She did not try to explain that by now Eliza would be speaking Shawnee and long habituated to the ways of her tribe. She might even of her own free will have formed an alliance and birthed childen. She could only be ransomed at the cost of a broken heart.

Nancy turned to her eldest son, Ethan, who accepted her charge in the name of something he called the family's honor. He gathered one hundred dollars from the settlement at large—every man felt compelled to offer something—and assembled a group to ride to a Shawnee camp, rumored to be situated near the Ohio. They returned eight days later to report the camp burned to the ground and the Shawnee dispersed with their captive. Nancy continued to plead for another attempt, but the trail was long cold and many believed that the girl was either dead or lost to Christianity.

Nancy was aging, bowed and broken by her many births and decades of work. She vowed that she would not die until she had been reunited with her lost daughter. After much beseeching, Ethan collected an additional fifty dollars from the settlement at large and assembled another band to ride across the Ohio and search the Shawnee towns on the western bank.

Eighteen days later, hallooing and kicking their horses, the men rode back into the settlement. Margaret helped her mother to her feet and they went with several neighbors to witness the return.

Eliza slid down from her horse—she was riding astride, not bundled behind the back of one of the men—and stared at the gaping villagers. She seemed amazed when Nancy hobbled forward to embrace her.

Although Eliza was comely and clearly of a marriageable age, something about her—perhaps the frankness of her stare or the straightness of her spine—caused Margaret to doubt that another Michael Erskine would step forward.

"Fetch the other children," her mother told her in a quivering voice, but when they finally came to greet their long-lost sister, she stared at them without recognition and accepted their embraces with obvious reluctance.

Margaret tried to reassure the young woman in Shawnee, then led her to their mother's cabin. Nancy followed them, saying "So you've come home at last, my daughter, and now I can lay down this weary life and die in peace." And indeed, before the week was out, she had taken to her bed.

"The Indian girl," as the villagers called her, stayed by her mother during the seven weeks of her slow dying, seeming to recognize, finally, their kinship. She bathed Nancy's feverish forehead with cool water and sometimes rested her face beside her mother's on the pillow. When Nancy died, her lost daughter raised the mournful howling Margaret remembered from the Shawnee camps until the preacher rushed in and laid his big hand over her mouth.

After she had seen her mother laid to rest in the little burial ground, the Indian girl returned to the cabin. She scoured it thoroughly, then burned her mother's clothes and soiled bedding. Margaret did not attempt to help her; she knew this ritual was providing her sister with an essential bit of comfort. And when the cross the preacher had planted over Nancy's grave disappeared one dark night, Margaret said nothing to quiet the villagers' murmuring. In any event, she thought, the burial ground was already so crowded with crosses, mainly those of babies and children, that their mother's unmarked grave was well-attended by the silent dead.

In the months and years that followed, the Indian girl was only seen to leave the cabin to fetch water, attend to her necessities in the woods, or work her little garden. Margaret surmised that she also dug roots and collected berries. Now and then one of the neighbors would lay a dead rabbit or squirrel on the doorstep, but no one attempted to speak to the young woman or persuade her to leave the cabin.

Margaret, stopping by now and then, spoke to her in Shawnee, hoping to provide some comfort, but the young woman did not appear to welcome Margaret's attention. Much occupied with her own half-grown brood, Margaret visited her sister less and less, persuading herself that the sight of smoke rising from the cabin chimney meant that its inhabitant was alive and to some degree well.

CHAPTER TWENTY-FIVE

ARGARET'S FOUR ERSKINE children were growing
swiftly into tall strangers. All of the boys, she thought, took
strongly after their father, with penetrating dark eyes under
inky eyebrows, long sharp noses, and thin lips often set in a line.
Her daughter, Jane, was a softer version, with blond hair falling
to her shoulders and a spritely humor that attracted the atten-
tions of Hugh Elmwood Caperton, a prosperous and respected
member of the community. Jane and Hugh were the first in that
generation to marry.

Before any amount of time had passed, it seemed to Margaret,
marriages were happening and children were being born. Falling
asleep at night, she carefully listed all her grandchildren's names:
Catherine, John Paulee (her long-dead husband's only name-
sake), another William, then another Jane, then an Eleanor, Allen,
another Michael, and, finally, an Agnes.

Her daughter, Jane, mother of Allen (in time a U.S. Senator),
Margaret Melinda, Mary Jane, Lewis, Elizabeth (called Betsey)
George, and James. Her husband, Hugh Caperton, built a big house
across the valley from Walnut Grove and called it Elmwood. It
stood under the hill where the graveyard was laid out; Margaret had
already chosen her spot at the crest, with a wide view of the valley
and the growing town in the distance.

John, long since grown to manhood, visited from time to time to see his mother, but he never lingered long. He had no chosen profession, having rejected the law, and his uncle was no longer willing to house and feed him. Margaret did not protest when John told her that he was leaving with a group of fur trappers to travel west to the banks of the Yellowstone River, where there was a chance, still, of finding a good number of otters to kill and skin. The traders were no longer eager to buy beaver since the pelts were not wanted for men's hats—the fashion had changed—but otter was beginning to be called for to trim women's cloth coats.

During the following two years, she received three letters brought by travelers who had crossed her son's path in that far-off place, then nothing. She knew well what that meant.

Finally, word came that John had been killed on the Yellowstone by a band of Mandan Indians unwilling to share their hunting grounds with what they thought was a group made up entirely of white men.

His body was buried somewhere in that territory. Margaret found herself wondering why the misfortune he had endured for his entire short life—the cruel issue, never resolved, of his parentage—had not somehow protected him from the Mandan, ancient allies of the Shawnee.

She did not mourn for long. There was no form for it, no burial service, no grave to visit with a handful of flowers. And she knew in her heart that John was free at last of the suspicions that had clouded his life.

As time passed, the enormous brood of grandchildren and great-grandchildren was a source of comfort to Michael Erskine, who often smoked his pipe by the big stone fireplace in the Walnut

Grove parlor, telling stories to anyone who would listen of the old days of danger and hardship.

Only one grandson, Jane's son Allen Caperton, captured Margaret's attention. He rode across the valley often of an evening, hallooing as he galloped up the hill to Walnut Grove. Margaret would bestir herself to throw another log on the fire and set the kettle on the hob for tea.

Smelling of horse and his own fierce sweat, Allen would take a seat beside her. As he accepted his cup, he often asked her to tell the tale of her years with the Shawnee.

Margaret hesitated to begin. The decades that had passed had not dimmed her memory but had made her reluctant to tell a story most listeners only found alarming.

At last one winter afternoon in her eighty-sixth year, she watched as Allen drew a notebook out of his jacket pocket and reached for the inkwell.

"Begin, Grandmama," he said, his voice reminding her of his grandfather's. "Time grows short."

Margaret knew that it did.

She sighed deeply and leaned back in her rocker, clasping her age-spotted hands in her lap. Her hands recorded many years of labor, but that, she knew, was not the story Allen wanted. Perhaps telling of her captivity from the beginning when she was a young wife with a baby in front of her on the saddle was the only way to the reconciliation with her kin that had always eluded her. Perhaps in time to come readers would believe her account and the hatred that had done so much finally to drive the Shawnee from the Ohio Country would be to some slight degree abated.

She remembered the sentences near the conclusion of *The Pilgrim's Progress* that she had learned by heart so many years ago: "I see myself now at the end of my journey; my toilsome days are ended."

Then, as Allen dipped his pen and held it suspended over the first page of his notebook, Margaret Handley Paulee Erskine began:

"On the twenty-third day of September in 1779, we set out West for the fertile lands of Kentucky."

ABOUT THE AUTHOR

S ALLIE BINGHAM is the author of seventeen books, including *Little Brother: A Memoir, Treason: A Sallie Bingham Reader, The Silver Swan: In Search of Doris Duke*, and *Passion and Prejudice: A Family Memoir*. She is winner of the 2023 Thomas Wolfe Fiction Prize, *Foreword Magazine*'s Gold Medal in Fiction for *Mending: New & Selected Short Stories*, and her work has been included in *Best American Short Stories* and the *PEN/O. Henry Prize Stories*. She has received fellowships from Yaddo, MacDowell, and the Virgina Center for the Creative Arts. Bingham is founder of the Kentucky Foundation for Women and The Sallie Bingham Center for Women's History at Duke University. She was publisher of *The American Voice* from 1989 to 1998 and book editor at *The Courier Journal* from 1983 to 1989. She lives in Santa Fe.